ATTICUS

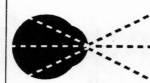

ATTICUS

Ron Hansen

Thorndike Press • Thorndike, Maine

Published in 1996 by arrangement with HarperCollins Publishers, Inc.

Grateful acknowledgment is made to the following for permission to reprint selections in this book:

Excerpts from *Pre-Columbian Literatures of Mexico* by Miguel León-Portilla. Translated from the Spanish by Grace Lobanov and Miguel León-Portilla. Copyright © 1969 by the University of Oklahoma Press.

"Eye-Opener" from *The Collected Poetry of Malcolm Lowry* by Malcolm Lowry. Copyright © 1992 by the Estate of Malcolm Lowry. Reprinted by permission of Sterling Lord Literistic, Inc.

"Here Comes the Sun." Words and Music by George Harrison. Copyright © 1969 Harrisongs Ltd. International Copyright Secured. All Rights Reserved.

"Tú, Sólo Tú" by Felipe Valdes Leal. Copyright © 1949 by Promotora Hispano Americana de Musica. Copyright Renewed. Administered by Peer International Corporation. International Copyright Secured.

Thorndike Large Print ® Americana Series.

The tree indicium is a trademark of Thorndike Press.

The text of this Large Print edition is unabridged. Other aspects of the book may vary from the original edition.

Set in 16 pt. Times New Roman.

Printed in the United States on permanent paper.

Library of Congress Cataloging in Publication Data

Hansen, Ron, 1947–
Atticus : a novel / Ron Hansen.
    p.   cm.
  ISBN 0-7862-0728-0 (lg. print : hc)
   1. Fathers and sons — Colorado — Fiction. 2. Adult children — Death — Fiction. 3. Ranchers — Colorado — Fiction. 4. Murder — Mexico — Fiction. 5. Large type books. I. Title.
[PS3558.A5133A93 1996b]
813′.54—dc20   96-17590

to Jim and Karen Shepard

The author wishes to thank the John Simon Guggenheim Foundation, the Lyndhurst Foundation, and the University of California, Santa Cruz, for their generous assistance during the writing of this book.

Colorado

ONE

His name was Atticus Cody. He was sixty-seven years old and a cattleman without cattle, the owner of six oil rigs and four hundred forty acres of high plains and sandhills in Antelope County, Colorado. And Atticus was on One Sock in December weather that was just above zero when he looked up at a coupling on his Lufkin oil jack and caught sight of two white suns in the gray winter sky. Weeds and sage were yellow against the snow and the snow strayed over the geography as though recalling how it was to be water. And just above the nodding horsehead pump were the sun and its exact copy, like the moons of another planet. One Sock champed on his wide spade bit and high-stepped up from a deep patch of snow but otherwise seemed unperplexed. Atticus squinted up at the suns and thought to himself, *You have lived sixty-seven years and now you have seen a sundog.*

At five he did what he always did at five. Atticus cracked the frail pane of ice on the horse-water tank and forked horse silage onto the fresh snow for Pepper and One Sock. He took off his yellow gloves in the tack room and shook chicken-flavored cornmeal into the house cat's tin bowl and watched as Skeezix softly crouched on the floor and crunched hard pellets of food. Crows were pecking at saltine crackers that he had crushed on the kitchen porch, and flits of snow were skewing under the fluttering yard light; and a yellow taxi was heading away from the front of his white two-story house.

Atticus hurried out and yelled, "Who's there?" but heard no reply. And by the time he got to the house porch, whoever it was had disappeared. Even his shoe prints were being winnowed away. Atticus replaced the green tarpaulin that had sagged off the gas tank and engine of his old Indian motorcycle, then he looked out at the night and a high plains landscape that was being gently simplified by the snow. His windburnt face was a cinnamon red, ice was on his gray mustache like candle wax, his fair blue eyes watered with cold. Atticus picked up the frozen Denver newspaper and opened the porch door without a key.

His forty-year-old son was sitting in his flight jacket on the green wingback chair inside, his hair bleached platinum and his handsome face tanned, just up from Mexico and grinning at his father's astonishment. Scott folded his hands behind his head and said with joy, "Merry Christmas!"

Atticus telephoned his firstborn son, but found out from Frank's wife that he was still at a budget-committee hearing at the Colorado state legislature.

"You'll have to face me alone then," Scott said.

Atticus just smiled and fried pork chops and hash browns in an iron skillet while his son opened a chilled bottle of California wine. Atticus tore up some red lettuce for a salad and when he saw his son holding the fancy electric carving knife heard himself say, "Don't play with that." Like he was fourteen. At supper Atticus talked pleasantly about family and farming and old friends who had died, the funny things that Frank's little Jennifer was saying these days, Frank's fine speech about responsibility and self-discipline to the Antelope Boys' Club, Frank's informed letter to the editor in *Oil and Gas Journal*, the new sixty-horse Ajax engine that Atticus and his older son had hauled onto one rig. Eating in silence, Scott took it all in like a hired hand, like he used to in high school when he treated their family suppers as his penance. And now he hardly spoke except to say when asked that he was house-sitting for friends in Quintana Roo on the Mexican Caribbean.

"Which town?"

"Resurrección. Twenty miles south of

Cancún. Eighteenth-century mission town tarted up for the tourists."

"We got a Lutheran church here by that name. Resurrection."

His son smiled with a familiar irritation. "You do always look for the local angle."

Atticus folded his napkin as if his next question was one of indifference to him. "Who are these friends you're house-sitting for?"

"You want their names or their occupations?"

"Want to know if your judgment's improved since Key West."

"That was one guy in a house of six people."

"And he's in prison, isn't he."

His son's stare was cold as he said, "Unfortunately, these friends are halfway criminal, too."

"Criminal how?"

"Can't say," Scott said, but he was smirking like he did in the old days when he told his father that his friends were Communists or heroin addicts or fresh out of reform school.

Atticus let it pass. "Are you going to stay in Mexico?"

"Even after I've worn out my welcome."

"Well, that'd be nice for us, just to know. You've moved fourteen times since you got outta college."

Scott said nothing but only hunkered low over his dinner plate, tipping his fingerprinted wineglass by the stem.

"England. New York City. Key West. That farm up in Vermont. I got a whole page for you in my address book."

"You left out the loony bin."

Atticus took up his knife and fiercely trimmed the fat from his pork chop. Hirsch Clinic. Signs for the simplest things: TODAY IS SUNDAY. SIT WHILE EATING. YOU ARE IN NEW YORK CITY. Hearing Scott tell his psychiatrist about his tries at suicide. Watching him teach finger painting. Hearing him inform his mother that the 503 on his hallway door was not an odd number, just an uneven one.

"Even today," Atticus said. "We're half sick because we haven't heard from you, and you surprise us from outta the blue when it was just as likely your older brother and I would have plans. You could of got a ride from Frank instead of hiring that taxi all that way. Was that a hundred dollars, or more?"

Scott held an affected white smile as he said, "I have this inheritance, you see. I have this fantastic trust fund that my father set up so he wouldn't go crazy with worry."

"I'd just like to see you get settled someplace."

"Well, I am."

"Well, good." Atticus pushed his dinner plate forward half a foot and carefully aligned his knife and fork across it. He had a flashback of Scott as a child in his high chair, chewing a cookie with great seriousness while he gazed out at the nothingness behind the kitchen window. *You wonder what he's thinking,* he'd said. "Writing poetry these days?"

"Nah. That was their idea."

Their. Them. Confined twice now, for three months each time. Atticus thought of Scottie at eight, talking to himself about the picture he was sketching with crayons on a torn grocery sack. And at fourteen with his paints, Serena behind him and gently smiling, a hand as soft as sunshine in his hair. "Well then," he asked. "Are you painting?"

"Yes."

"Sell anything?"

"I just *am,* Dad. You've got one son who's a huge success that any father'd be proud of, and you've got one son who's a slacker and using up your hard-earned cash on just getting by from week to week. Hell, I'm forty years old. You oughta be used to me being a failure by now."

Were Atticus to talk honestly, he thought, he'd say he was alone all the time and this was his son whom he loved and ached for, and heaven was where *he* was, and Atticus hated himself, as he always did, for insisting and teaching and holding up standards and seeming to want Scott to be him, when all he wanted was for Scott to be happy and to know he was loved and loved and loved. "Shall I change the subject?" he asked.

"Work it to death if you want."

Skeezix was on the floor heating vent, his green-yellow eyes only slits, his white cat paws tucked primly underneath his chest, surrendering himself to pleasure. Atticus asked, "Would you like some coffee?"

"You have whiskey?"

Atticus sighed but got up.

Then Atticus sat in his green wingback chair with a biography of Eisenhower, and Scott drank whiskey from a water glass and lay against a sofa pillow with a paperback version of the *Popol Vuh* open atop his gray Stanford T-shirt, his blue eyes nailed to the page with just that look of thrill and passion that he always got as a child. Even though he was forty years old, his hard body seemed much younger than that, but his bleached hair was hinting darker roots and his skin was weathered as brown as sorghum from a half year in the Caribbean sun. Atticus was trying to find features of himself in the high ridge of his cheekbones, his tightly shut mouth, his squint and quiet and carpenter's hands, when Scott caught his fatherly gaze with a sidelong glance and Atticus said, "Well, you appear pretty healthy."

"Wild living hasn't caught up with me yet."

"Are you still getting those headaches?"

"My head's all right."

Atticus thought for a while and then offered,

"I like this house a lot better with you in it."

"Uh huh."

Atticus opened up his book again. Eisenhower was first assigned to San Antonio, Texas, after West Point and in 1916 married Mamie Doud, whose father owned a meatpacking company in Denver. Atticus looked up. "I forgot to say. You see the sundog when you were flying in?"

Scott dully considered him. "I have no idea what you're talking about."

"You have just the right circumstances and a great big spot'll show up on the halo around the sun so it looks like you got two suns up there. Called a parhelion, if I got it right, the sundog is."

"Huh." Still flat on his back, Scott tilted whiskey into his mouth and put the glass on the floor.

"Well, it was a topic of conversation."

"You do try. I have to hand it to ya."

"Are we going to go on like this?"

"Like what?"

"Me being your prying old man and you being my ornery juvenile delinquent."

Scott held his hands behind his head and just stared at his father for a full minute. And then he said, "It's the flight. Culture shock. And frankly, there are those who'd say my hostilities have been held in check pretty well."

"But I have the benefit of knowing how you were brought up."

Scott faced him like furniture. "What, then?"

Atticus looked away to Serena's piano and all the framed pictures on it. "Well, I'd be real interested to hear how you spend your days."

"Nah, it's boring."

"Even so, I'd kinda like to hear."

"Wake up at ten or so, have coffee, walk to town for whatever mail there is and the English-language newspaper. Skin-dive or lift weights or jog on the beach. And then drinks and dinner out."

"You didn't have to mention the drinking."

"Ever think about getting a vice, Dad? You might find more tolerance for regular human beings."

"I got vices."

"Oh, right. You're addicted to order and cleanliness."

Atticus sought out a change of subject. "So who are your friends in Mexico?"

"Drunkards and expatriates. Writers, artists, some ex-movie people, cancer patients hunting miracle cures. Half the Americans in Resurrección are just middle-class retirees who can finally afford servants."

"You head down there for no particular reason?"

"No. I gave it some thought."

And there was a pause until Atticus asked, "Are you getting back together with Renata?"

"I hope so."

"She's there then?"

"Good guess."

Atticus smiled. "Well, I always liked her."

"Me too."

At six the next morning, Atticus got out the twelve-gauge shotgun for himself and his old sixteen-gauge for Scott, and he was sitting at the kitchen table, jotting out his Christmas shopping list, when his son jounced downstairs in his gray T-shirt and blue jeans, his eyes bloodshot from the whiskey and his hair in hurricane.

"Sleep okay?"

"An hour or two." Scott got a quart of orange juice from the refrigerator and sloshed it before drinking right from the carton. He spied the shotguns angled against the ironing board closet and regarded Atticus as he might a horribly outdated phrase of slang. *"Hunting?"*

"Don't have to," Atticus said. "Just thought you might've missed it."

"Hot-diggity."

"You still wear my size in everything?"

"Haven't changed much."

"Because I got some nice things hanging in the closet."

"And there must be people around here who'll be glad to have them."

Atticus held his stare.

Scott put Wonder bread in the toaster. "I'm

18

trying to get back to essentials, Dad. I'm trying to subtract things from my life.''

And then they sloshed through snow and hidden leaves in Frank's orchard and crashed through the high brittle cornstalks of the forty acres along the creek and quail blustered up from underfoot and pheasants sailed beautifully away. And Scott never even brought up his gun.

"Pretty out here," he said.

Atticus was at his underground workbench, using a screwdriver to tighten the shoe polisher on an old electric motor. Scott just stood there by the floor heater, acting as bored as a teenager, his breath fluttering grayly in the cold. Atticus seriously inquired, "Have I ever told you the difference between a bank and a beehive?"

His son smiled uncertainly and said no.

Atticus was trying the play on the shoe-polisher belt. "Well, a bank *pays* notes and a piano *plays* notes."

Scott just kept squinting at him in an askance way and then asked, "What about the beehive?"

Atticus merrily jabbed his son with the screwdriver and joked, "Why, that's where you get stung!"

Atticus painstakingly washed the dishes after dinner and Scott dried them and told him, "We'd had about a hundred feet of rain fall on us, but then it didn't rain at all for two days and the highways were being used again. And so I took my Volkswagen out to the jungle for the first time in a month and painted for half a day. And then I remembered that Renata expected me for dinner at six and it was already half past five and getting dark. I hurried into the Volkswagen and took a shortcut into town, skidding wildly in mud, and going way too fast for the road. Suddenly I rushed up on a half-dozen Mayan kids in their finest white shirts and pants, probably heading to work in the hotels. I honked the horn and they jumped from the road and frowned at me and there was this pothole filled with rainwater that my front tire plunged into, ramming hard, splashing their good clothes with muck. Their hands flew up and they yelled in fury and I thought I ought to go back and say how sorry I was. But then I thought about how late I was and how Renata would be fuming and how often their clothing must get ruined in the monsoon season. And I was gazing back in my rearview mirror to see them slapping the gunk from their shirts when the car slammed forward, *blam!*, into a trench of mud where the ground had crumbled away. I got the engine going again but then looked out the side window and saw the mud was as high as the door and my tires were turning fruitlessly in the slime. I shifted to first gear and then reverse, hoping to rock the car forward, but it only settled another inch or two. And I thought, *This is how God repays your thoughtlessness.* And then I looked up to see the Mayan kids were hulking around the Volkswagen, angrily peering in. But before I could say anything, I saw them bend from my sight and lift the Volkswagen and heave it forward until all four tires were on hard ground again and I could roll free of the mire. I got out of the car to thank them, but the kids walked ahead without saying a word. You have no idea how *Indian* that is."

On December twenty-third, Atticus skidded the great yellow barn door aside and One Sock and Pepper pranced inside to their wooden boxstalls, their horseshoes clopping on the floor planks. A hairy steam rose up from One Sock as Atticus took off the tack and gently scuffed a currycomb along his glossy chestnut back. Scott scooped oats into a tin bucket and said, "I don't remember the measurements."

"A half quart of oats, four pounds of hay. And put some pebbles in with the oats or she'll feed too fast and she'll scour." Atticus watched his son step inside the stall and patiently hold the oat bucket up to Pepper just as he would years ago, as though the pinto couldn't swallow uphill. Atticus said, "Hay first; but that's okay."

"She's very hungry," Scott said.

"She's just flirting with ya. She probably

wants sympathy. Wants to poison you against One Sock." Atticus squatted with a horse blanket in order to dry the snow from One Sock's flanks and quarters, and he heard Scott soothingly talking to Pepper in Mayan, words like *ichpuchtla* and *patli* and *yol.* Atticus stayed as he was for a while, trying not to listen, his blue eyes on the straw, and then he stood up and trued the green horse blanket over One Sock's withers and croup. His son's eyes were shut and he was pressing his nose into the pinto's long jaw when Atticus asked, "You okay?"

Scott's glance caught sight of his father's misgivings and he grinned. "Hell, I'm crazy as a loon."

Atticus hooked the currycomb on a nail and slowly walked out of One Sock's stall to the oat sack. "Are you taking your medication?"

"You mean right now?"

"Ever."

Scott sagged against a railing, blowing heat into his fingers. "The trouble is, lithium makes me so dopey that I have to pat my face to know where my mouth is. And there are side effects, too. Hand tremors, slurring, blackouts, fatigue."

Atticus scooped oats into another tin bucket. "We could go into town and have your prescription —"

"My *prescription's* just right, Dad. I have pills that make me harmless and stupid, pretty much the kind of guy who sits on a bench and feeds croutons to the pigeons. I'd rather walk in a southerly wind and not know a hawk from a handsaw."

Atticus carried the tin bucket to One Sock and held it for him until all the feed was gone.

The Codys gathered together for Christmas Eve in the great, white, three-story house that Atticus grew up in, that was inherited by his older brother and was owned now by State Senator Frank L. Cody and his wife, Marilyn. She had given birth to three girls and a boy and was the fourth of six children, so there wasn't room at the dining room table for all the company, and her brothers Merle and Butch and Marvin hunched toward their TV trays from the sofa, and Scott, in spite of many pleas and objections, chose to eat at a card table with his nieces. Oyster stew and crackers would be served, then Marilyn's Waldorf salad and spinach quiche, Esther's ambrosia, Cassie's scalloped potatoes with Kraft cheese slices, and Connie's stalks of broccoli in a hollandaise sauce, but before all that there were green magnums of a fancy champagne that Scotty had traveled all the way into Denver for just that afternoon. "Well, I be go to hell," said Marvin. "Denver."

"We call this nose tickier," Merle told Scott.

"Champagne gives me the most gruesome

headaches," said Esther.

A few minutes later Frank herded his four-year-old over to her Uncle Scott and blandly asked, "You sip any of that Veuve Clicquot, Jennifer?"

She saw her father's cue and nodded.

"What's your opinion of it?"

She hesitated and then recited, "It lacked a certain *je ne sais quoi*." And she flinched when she heard sudden laughter from all her uncles and aunts.

"Oh, you, Frank," Cassie said. "Did you put her up to that?"

Then the family found their places. All held hands as Frank recited the blessing before the meal, and at the finish Marilyn mentioned Serena: "We still miss you, Mom."

Children looked at Atticus and at Scott.

Then Frank held forth from the head of the dining room table, being funny and hectoring and omniscient in his English suit and European tie and his ring from the Colorado School of Mines. Atticus heard later from Marilyn that Scott watched with jealousy as Atticus and Frank huddled together over black coffee to talk about income tax write-downs on their Cody Petroleum partnership and figure out how many heifers the cattle operation ought to breed in the fall.

At eight o'clock Midge played Santa Claus underneath the giant pine tree in the teal, high-ceilinged living room, giving out a great stack of presents. Luciano Pavarotti grandly sang carols, and pretty wrapping paper was loudly torn, and children's toys rattled and zinged and nickered across the carpet. Atticus carefully peeled away the red paper on his present from Scott and popped open a box containing a Swiss wristwatch that, according to Connie, was worth one thousand dollars. Atticus scowled and asked his son, "Are you trying to throw your money away?" but Scott was sticking a green cigar in his mouth and hugely grinning into Butch's videotape camera and saying, "Isn't this great?" Then Atticus jiggled a grandchild on his knee as Scott got his gift from his older brother and ogled a handsome Winchester twelve-gauge shotgun with checkering on its hardwood stock. "Wow! Heat! Won't those *banditos* be surprised!"

Atticus stared with irritation at Frank, who justified the shotgun by saying, "I heard Dad got you out hunting again. And I figured you probably had havelina and deer and poisonous snakes down there."

His kid brother sighted down the dark barrel and said, "Yeah. In the jungle. Snakes are called yellowbites."

Atticus hefted a heavy box from behind his chair and presented it to Scott. "You may not want to haul it down to Mexico with you on the plane. I'll ship it maybe."

Scott hastily tore off the green wrapping paper just as he did as a child, and he blushed when he saw an off-brand cassette player. "Wow, Dad! Thanks! A Radiola!"

"Earl — you remember Earl at the hardware — he told me it plays just as good as a Sony or an Aiwa and the others, and Radiola's an American brand."

"Well, I'm proud to do my part for the war effort, Dad."

"Didn't put batteries in it. I figured you had electric in that shack of yours or you wouldn't be painting at night."

"My neighbors don't have it, but I do."

Atticus said, "You got a mike built right in it so you can record, too. What I planned on was to have you mail us tapes of yourself talking into it. And we'd do the same for you, of course, any time we have family occasions. Wouldn't be like we're all so far away."

Scott grinned hugely at him and said, "I *love* Christmas!"

There was talk in the air when Atticus woke up for Mass on Christmas Day; and Indian speech that was like the hissing, popping noise of flames creeping across damp wood. And then there was silence. Atticus got into his clothes and stood just outside his son's upstairs room, trying to decide if he ought to go in and then gently nudging the

26

door ajar and holding there before he understood that Scott was gone, the gray smoke was incense, and the harsh smell that of whiskey. His son had taken Mary and Joseph and the Wise Men from the Nativity set in the dining room and put birthday candles around them on his schoolboy desk. And underneath them on the oak floor Scott had arranged a half dozen more birthday candles on bricks that he'd blessed with Jack Daniel's.

Atticus walked into the kitchen and saw the ceiling light was still on and the teapot was simmering hot water on top of the stove. A Christmas snow put round caps on the fence posts and lay in the jack oak like socks and mittens. Scott's shoe prints slued bluely across the yard to the yellow barn and then to the quarter-mile windbreak of loblolly pines and crabapple trees where Atticus kept the older farm machinery. Atticus put on his Army Air Corps jacket and cattleman's hat and went out. Cold snow crunched beneath his gray cowboy boots with the toothgrind noise of cattle chewing. Jewels of sunlight sparked from the whiteness everywhere. And there under the green pine limbs was the red hay baler, the yellow crawler tractor and bulldozer blade, the plows and reaper and cultivator that were going orange with rust, and the milk-white Thunderbird just as it was sixteen years ago when Scott took Serena to the store. The high speed of the accident had destroyed one headlight and crumpled up the right fender and hood like writing paper meant to be thrown away. The right wheel tilted on its axle as though it had not been fully bolted on, and the rubber tire shredded from it like black clothing scraps.

Atticus walked around to the driver's side and opened the door. The iron complained at his pull but Scott did not look up, he stayed as he was, in his father's red plaid hunting coat, just sitting there, one wrist atop the big steering wheel, his right hand gingerly touching the windshield glass where it was crushed and spiderwebbed on the passenger's side. A milky light was filtering through the half-inch screen of snow. Atticus asked, "You okay?"

Scott pressed his cold-reddened fingertips into a crack and said, "Wondered if her hair was still there. Crows must be nesting with it."

Atticus could only say, "I should of got rid of this car years ago."

Scott dropped his hands and forearms into his lap. He said, "A great thing about Spanish is that there's so little responsibility in it. You don't have to take the blame. You don't say 'I cracked the plate.' You say 'The plate cracked itself.' " Scott paused and just stared at the grayly misted speedometer as if there were ugly pictures there.

And Atticus said, "You don't say you killed your mother. You say your mother was killed."

Atticus nipped off a green cigar's end and spit it into the wastepaper basket as Scott stooped toward the gas flame of the stovetop to get his own cigar going. Then Scott got his bottle of Armagnac and they walked out into Christmas night.

The moon was high and the night was sugared with stars. An Antelope County road plow had again scraped the mail routes to a shine, and zero cold made the snow underfoot as hard as linoleum. Scott tipped up the Armagnac and Atticus waited and stopped himself from giving his known opinions about it. Soon Scott was walking again and saying, "She once strolled into the dining hall at Hirsch in nothing but a bedsheet."

"You're talking about Renata?"

"Right. Attendants tried to herd her out but Renata did this fantastic pirouette, the sheet swooshing off her, all the guys howling, and she's standing there in the altogether with the orderlies rushing to haul her out when she flings her hands high and says, 'But people like me this way!' "

"She fine now?"

"Oh yeah; better than me. She tried acting in New York for a while — that's as crazy as she's been."

"Huh," Atticus said.

"She's got a room in this pink villa owned by a Brit."

"In Mexico."

"Yep. The friend is Stuart Chandler. Runs the English-language bookstore, grows orchids, holds forth on sundry topics. He's the American consul there."

They walked fifty yards without further comment, and then Scott teetered as he tainted the road with gray ash. "Enjoying your cigar, Dad?"

Atticus turned and talked through his teeth. "Isn't lit."

"Like mine a little hotter than that."

"It's nearly tolerable this way."

Wheeling snow twisted by in a sudden gust and then flattened on a highway that shone in the moonlight like wax. Atticus heard Scott finish a sentence with, "Went native for a while and got into shamanism."

"Renata did?"

"Me." His son looked at his cigar and then huddled over it as he lit it again.

"You have your own religion."

"Shamanism isn't instead of; it's in addition to."

"Why's everything you do have to be so different? Wouldn't it be easier to just do things like they have been done and not fuss so much inventing?"

"I *have* been a trial to you, haven't I?"

"Well, that's just being a father, mostly."

Scott shifted his green cigar in his mouth and withdrew inside Atticus's black cashmere overcoat. After a while he said, " 'The air bites shrewdly.' "

"Are you quoting?"

"Hamlet."

Atticus tugged off a kid leather glove and offered his left hand to the north wind. "About five degrees."

Scott tilted the Armagnac bottle again and tottered up against a high snowbank as he drank. He then capped the bottle top with his thumb, put his cigar back in his mouth, and sat heavily in the snow so that his hips were deeper than his knees. He was surprised to be there for a second and then simpered like a dunce.

"You're just a tiny bit *borracho,* son."

"And you're being real agreeable about it. Expected you to be more fractious." Atticus got the whiskey bottle from him and Scott gave his blue eyes to the night sky, the cigar centered between his teeth. "See up there? Ursa Major?"

"You mean the Big Dipper."

"Exactly. The Mayans call that Seven Macaw."

"Hmm."

"Also, there's a story about the Pleiades being Four Hundred Boys who got too drunk on *chicha*

31

and were sent up there when they died. Mayans call their corn whiskey 'sweet poison.' "

"Helluva brand name."

"You're darn tootin'. We oughta copyright it, put a little circle around the *R*." Scott offered his left arm and his father attached his own to it, lifting his son up from the snow. And then Atticus was walking the quarter mile back to the house and Scott Cody was just behind him saying, "Heart of sky, heart of earth, one true god, green road."

Weeks later, Atticus walked out to the mailbox and found an airmail envelope from Mexico. But inside was a letter from Scott to Frank that thanked him again for the shotgun and talked about other worrisome things.

After a late night of drinking and danc-
ing at The Scorpion, the Delta Gamma
from California tells me that she's bad
and she'll wreck my life, she's done it to
a slew of guys. She's falling apart as she
tells me she wants to love just one person,
and for that person to love just her. She's
twenty and stewed and majoring in Thea-
ter Arts, so I have reason to believe she's
being dramatic, but then she's in my lap —
we're in my VW, so this is no mean feat —
telling me what a mistake this would be, but

32

to take her now, here, quickly. Be my fantasy, she says. And I know I am in way over my head.

And then there's Renata. I have followed her from town to town for more than fifteen years. She calls it stalking, I call it love. She throws me a bone now and then — a tryst, an oh-what-the-hell affair — but more often she stamps her foot and shoos me. I have been getting the go-aways lately and it's beginning to feel done, over, finished. We talked when I got back and she told me she was, for the very first time, in love — meaning no offense, of course, though it did add a caustic charge to the midnight cigar and too-many whiskeys that my friends put down in front of me.

I know these two stories go together — less than forty-eight hours separate them — and in both I was the stooge. On the phone with Renata I tried not to say, "Try to get it right this time," but that was there, and I think that I have lost something, and I lost it before Renata, lost it as far back as the accident. This is not a complaint; I just have no clue.

Confessions like this are maybe not what older brothers like to hear, but I know you'll be flattered by it. I hear the three favorite words are not "I love you" but "What's your opinion?'' A guy I know here chides me for being softheaded. We're playing pool at the American Bar. And I am sailing on Coronas and shots of tequila. The Warriors and Chicago are on cable and the furthest gone exiles are hooting at some nifty moves in the paint. Who's that singing on the jukebox? Whitney Houston? I love that song. I hold out my heart for dissection and see this guy Reinhardt looking at me like I'm a mark, like I've got "Kick me" pinned on the back of my shirt. Renata's walking all over you, that sort of thing.

Long meaningless strolls, holding hands, chips and salsa by the pool, skin against skin, how about a back rub? — it's full of intimacy and self revelation, and I feel lost without it. Love in my shoes. Love in the hand on my thigh. Love hanging around like a good waiter when we dine by candlelight. Want it, need it, gotta have it. I'm forty years old and the clock's still running.

All I can do now is paint. There are feelings then, big and troublesome. But with the other stuff, I have no idea. I'm trying my hand at patience. I try your patience, too, I know. Try to remember that every President has a flake in the family.

Scott

Late that night, Atticus got a phone call from Frank. "Dad? I got a letter to you from Scott by mistake."

"Oh?" Atticus said. "What's it say?"

"He thanks you for the Radiola. Says he's working hard and he's off the sauce. Half page is all. Seems fine."

"Well, that's good to hear."

On a Wednesday in February, Atticus listened to the public radio station for company as he cooked up an onion stew and poured it over rye bread, slowly eating it in the dining room with *The Denver Post* propped up on his milk glass. Marilyn would be stopping by at noon with her own philosophies of good housekeeping, so Atticus only rinsed off the pan, the plate, the milk glass and spoon, then completed some government accounting forms at his rolltop desk and went upstairs at nine. Howling winds rattled the windowpanes and piped like a hot teapot at every wooden gap in the house. His upstairs radio was tuned to opera, *La Bohème*, and his wife was still not there. He slanted into heaped pillows in his pajamas in order to read petroleum reports and then woke up with the side lamp on and loose pages sloppily pitched to the floor. He couldn't get back to sleep, so he put on his Black Watch tartan robe and slippers and walked through all the upstairs rooms, stopping especially in Scott's.

His paint brushes were in a red coffee can just as they'd been for over twenty years and his childhood sketches and watercolors overlapped on the walls, but Atticus could no longer smell the linseed oil and turpentine and paints that used to mean his son to him, he could only smell whiskey and tobacco and the harsh incense of his shaman rites.

Atticus turned up the kitchen radio so he could hear people give their hasty opinions on a nighttime phone-in show while he peeled a Washington apple at the stoop window and looked out toward the machine shed. Horizontal snow was flying through the halo of the green yard light and carrots of ice were hanging from the roof's iron gutters. Atticus ate apple slices off the sharp blade of his paring knife. Without knowing why, he looked to the pantry, and just then a milk pitcher slipped off its hook and crashed onto the pantry floor.

Hours after sunup Atticus carried a tin pail of hot water out to One Sock and Pepper, scooped oats into a pan, and then crouched quietly in a stall corner, looking up at the horses' slow chewing. A sparrow flew in an upper window and got lost in the night of the barn, slashing among the high rafters and pigeon roosts and loudly rapping into a penthouse window before swooping low enough to veer out through the great door and rise up.

Atticus petted One Sock along the withers and went outside to his snow-topped Ford pickup for his daily trip to the Antelope truck stop. And then he got the feeling that the house telephone was ringing. He argued with himself about whether he ought to go to it or no. The truck's ignition ground like an auger in iron and the engine caught and Atticus gave it gas for half a minute, looking out at the yellow barn and silo and unhenned coop, Serena not putting eggs in her gray sweater pockets as the white chickens strutted away, Serena's peacock not jerking its glare at the dog and making its glamorous tail display. Weather reports on the truck radio said the temperature was up to fifteen degrees, but his bare fingers were still pretty sore, so he got out and went back inside to get his yellow gloves.

Atticus stopped by the house telephone and looked at it, and the telephone began ringing. He hesitated and then picked up the receiver and heard Renata Isaacs. She first reminded him of who she was. "I haven't forgotten," he said. She said she was calling from Resurrección. And then she talked to him about Scott. Atticus pulled over a spindle chair, and she explained the circumstances. She was trying not to cry. Atticus was sitting there, not saying anything he meant to, and wiping a porthole in the steamed windowpane with one yellow glove. The truck's engine was running at high speed, and the smoke from the tailpipe was shaping gray people that a hard wind ripped away. She said how terrible she felt, she was as upset as he was, she hadn't known his son was that depressed. Atticus accepted her sympathy and he wrote down her telephone number and then he lost himself until he heard her hang up on the other end. Atticus couldn't get up without gripping the crosspiece on the spindle chair. He went out and switched off the truck's ignition, and then he telephoned Frank in his Antelope office, giving him the news.

Upstairs in Scott's room was a green wall shingled with high school and college paintings, all created in those happy times when everything that Scotty touched seemed to turn into a picture. Atticus stared at the portrait of himself as he was twenty years ago, forty-seven and finding wealth in oil, his hair and great mustache a chestnut brown, his blue eyes checkered by the stoop's windowpanes, the April sunlight like buttermilk, just back from Mass in his blood-red tie and a hard-as-cardboard shirt that was so blazingly white it glowed. His son had titled the picture "Confidence."

Atticus sat at his son's oak desk and pulled out a lower right-hand drawer jammed with manila folders upon which Scott had printed, in a fine draftsman's style, Art Schools, Banking, Credit

Cards, Fellowships and Grants, Medical, Taxes, and Vita. As organized as an engineer. Atticus lifted out the Vita file and slumped back in a tilting chair to page through it. Eight years of report cards from Saint Mary's Grade School were on top, then white First Honors cards and typed grade slips from Regis High School in Denver, followed by his senior transcript from the office of the registrar at Stanford University. The Royal College of Art in England had sent correspondence to accept him, then provided the financial terms of his stay, and then forwarded a letter in which one of his British teachers appraised Scott's failing studio work over the year: "Skillful, safe, formulaic," he'd written, and "You lack nothing in terms of technique, but is it art or illustration?" Scott had four photocopies of an old curriculum vitae that he used to send out in hopes of employment as an art instructor, that provided a home address in care of Atticus Cody in order to avoid mention of the New York hospital he was staying in. Under "teaching experience," Scott had recorded giving art therapy at Hirsch Clinic and then still-life painting sessions at the Self-Help Center. His age was then thirty-three, and his health, he'd said, was fine. And to that information, he'd added in pen on all four copies: "I dress myself, do not act out, and am never tardy. I believe we all should help one another find our controllers. We all have functions in the machine."

Alongside his Vita file was a sheaf of his poems from one of his times at the clinic. The first one went:

> Here it's fall.
> I feel no pain.
> I hate you all.
> I'll kill again.

Atticus heard the kitchen door open and he put the files away. And he was dabbing a handkerchief to his eyes when he heard Marilyn in the hallway.

"Dad?" she called.

"Good morning!"

Frank's wife hit the light switch as she walked inside the room in her navy blue parka and ski pants and gray overboots, his infant grandson against her right shoulder, a blue blanket capping Adam's head. Marilyn's aviator glasses grayed with the temperature change. She said, "Frank's talking to the American Embassy in Mexico City. We'll have trouble getting his body back right away."

Atticus got his grandson from her and grinned down as he gentled and cradled the boy. Adam struggled to look at the overhead light, at the ceiling, and then gazed for a long time at his grandfather's big gray mustache.

Marilyn lifted her aviator glasses and pressed a balled-up tissue to her eyes and nose and then pushed the tissue inside her parka sleeve. Her lipstick was slightly awry. She looked at Scott's desk. "Are you hunting for something?"

"Explanations."

She smiled uncertainly and said, "I have that new priest from Saint Mary's here."

"Good."

"First *The Denver Post* looked us up. And then the *Rocky Mountain News*. Him being the brother to a state senator. Woman in Mexico called them, I guess. Seems to me that's the family's job."

"Well, she probably figured she knew first-hand how it happened."

"I knew his birthday and high school and college, but that was just about it. You know so much about your family, and all the obituaries seem to want is dates."

Adam reached up and patted Atticus on a wind-burnt cheek that was scattered with lines. Atticus kissed the boy's tiny hand and said, "Expect Frank's taking it pretty hard."

"Well, it was the shotgun he gave him at Christmas. We always thought, though . . . you know, that he'd put all that behind him."

Marilyn collected her son again as Atticus got up from the chair. He said, "How would you like some coffee?"

* * *

The priest was sitting coatless at the kitchen table, fresh out of the seminary and maybe forty pounds overweight, and Atticus couldn't remember his name. Marilyn put through a telephone call to her husband and was handed over to his secretary, her cousin Cassie, while Frank finished his talk with a friend in the State Department. Marilyn dipped the mouthpiece. "You'll have to go through the American consul in Resurrección. She's getting me the number."

"I have it," Atticus said. "Look on that pad there."

Marilyn gazed at Renata Isaacs's home telephone number and then at Atticus as Frank's secretary gave her the American consul's number. "We have it, Cassie. Thanks."

Cassie handed her back to Frank and there was talk about a funeral home. Atticus crossed his arms by the coffeepot, watching the light brown explosions in the glass thimble on top. The percolating coffee was becoming important to him. Marilyn was put on hold again. She looked at Atticus and said, "You ought to go down, Dad."

"I expect."

The priest asked, "You know Spanish?"

"Word or two," Atticus said. "Mexican workers used to head up to Antelope after the cantaloupe harvest in Rocky Ford, and I'd usually have a job or two they could help me with. About all

I remember now is hammer is *el martillo* but a sledgehammer is *el macho.*"

"I could give you my Spanish phrase book if it's any help."

"I have one. Anyway, it'll probably come back to me."

The priest stared at him and then his face seemed to freshen. "Wasn't Atticus the name of the father in *To Kill a Mockingbird*?"

"Oh? I hadn't heard that."

"Dad!" Marilyn said, and then turned to the priest. "Of course he's heard that. He's just putting you on."

"You know the boy in that book? The girl's only friend? That was Truman Capote."

"You don't say," Marilyn said. "Wasn't he charming?"

"Capote? Yes, he was."

Atticus stared intently at them both.

The priest rolled up the left sleeve of his red plaid shirt. "You haven't asked, but the Church presumes some profound mental upset in the case of a suicide. Especially when it's committed in this manner. Your son wouldn't be held responsible for his actions. And there's the problem of our prejudgment, too. We can't put limits on God's forgiveness."

Atticus got out a straw broom and swept up the milk pitcher that was in pieces and chips on the pantry floor. "How'd that happen?" Marilyn asked, but before Atticus could answer she was on the telephone again. She jotted further information on the notepad and hung up when she heard her husband's call-waiting tone.

The priest said, "I say that because you probably grew up in an age when a person who killed himself was denied Christian burial on the grounds that he was showing contempt for God's law."

"I see."

Atticus tapped cream into Serena's pink Dresden cups before pouring the coffee, and Marilyn sat across from the priest with Adam on her lap. She sipped a little coffee and rocked her boy and smelled the baby shampoo in his scalp. She said, "It doesn't seem possible, does it."

Atticus said, "She told me he went out to his studio to paint about one or so last night. And he seemed okay to her, a little frazzled and drifty, but not so she'd pay any extra attention. You know how Scott could be." Atticus stopped. His lips trembled and pulled down at the corners, and he held his mouth with his hand as he squinched his blue eyes closed.

"You go ahead, Dad," Marilyn said. "You've got every right."

Atticus wiped his eyes with a navy blue handkerchief. "Embarrassing myself here."

"Don't think about me," the priest said.

Atticus sipped his coffee, putting the cup on

the saucer with care. "This morning," he said, "Renata took his Volkswagen out to the house he worked in, I guess to find out if he was okay. She yelled in to him and Scott didn't yell back, so she just naturally went inside. You know, to see how things were. Scott —"

Atticus couldn't go on for a second and then the telephone rang and Marilyn gave it a second thought before getting up to answer it. Atticus got up from his spindle chair and limped over to the stoop window. More good people were expressing their sympathy. Marilyn said she knew Atticus appreciated their caring and their prayers. Atticus spied the outside temperature gauge: just twenty. Hotter in Mexico by fifty degrees or more. As soon as she hung up there was a telephone call from Cassie, and Marilyn asked, "Could you go down tonight, Dad?"

Atticus turned. Marilyn had covered the mouthpiece. "I guess I ought to," he said.

"You fly first-class, don't you?"

"Usually."

She arranged a night flight from Denver to Dallas to Mexico City, and a further connection to Mérida, but he'd have to get a bus to go farther east. The flights to Cancún were booked. And then the telephone rang again and she said, "Merle says he'll keep the horses at his place and drive you over to Denver."

"Don't want to put him —"

45

She handed him the phone.

"Merle? Don't want to put you out about the airport, but I would appreciate your looking out for my horses. And, you know, keeping an eye peeled. Expect Butch'll stay on top of the oil patch so you don't —"

Merle interrupted him in order to praise Scott and say how surprised and torn up he was to learn he'd passed away. And then he told Atticus a funny story about Scott operating a Case harvester one fall when he wasn't but twelve and pheasants kept flying up into the cab.

Atticus pictured it and smiled and then accepted Merle's sympathy and words of condolence and hung up the telephone. Marilyn was concentrating on her coffee and a brown scatter of the baby's animal crackers. She bumped Adam on her knee in order to keep him happy and, when Atticus moved from the telephone, looked up. "I had a good dream about Scott the other night. He was about six years old and riding Conniption, getting her to go right and left by yanking on her mane."

And then it was five, and Atticus walked out of the house in his gray Stetson cowboy hat and one of his navy blue suits, hefting just an overnight bag. Marilyn was by the stoop window helping her baby to flap his hand in good-bye. The green yard light blinked and glimmered and

46

then stayed on as Atticus gunned his truck and headed toward the highway and the pink horizon of sundown.

And it was New Year's Eve for Atticus again and Scott was slumped in the Ford pickup on the highway to the Denver airport, his hay-yellow hair skewed up against the side window, his index finger drawing eights on the steamed-up glass. An orange sun was just coming up. Hard sleet fishtailed across the highway and pinged like sand against the rocker panels. Scott hadn't slept and looked sort of slapped together. His lips were moving and his left hand was patting out a poem's meter on his knee. He apparently sensed Atticus peering at him and repeated " 'Thou art indeed just, Lord, if I contend with thee; but, sir, what I plead is just. Why do sinners' ways prosper? And why must disappointment' something something rhymes with contend.' "

"Especially like those somethings the guy put in there."

"Here's the complaint. 'Wert thou my enemy, O thou my friend, how wouldst thou worse, I wonder, than thou dost defeat, thwart me?' "

Atticus smiled. "Haven't heard 'wert' and 'dost' in a while."

" 'Oh, the' something 'thralls of lust do' I'm forgetting it 'thrive more than I that spend, sir, life upon thy cause.' You've got this priest who's given up sex, money, honors, the works, and as

47

a kind of compensation for that Hopkins hopes that God will at least help him out with spiritual consolations and poetry. Kind of a religious man's quid pro quo. And it doesn't pan out. All he feels is desert."

Atticus thought his son would be saying more, but when he looked to his right, Scott was just staring at the high plains outside. And it was like the days of the green GMC truck and the six o'clock rides southeast into town, Frank in a high school letterman's jacket and trying for a half-hour of sleep, and Scott just ten years old but yakking away like a grown-up, his lunchbox tightly held to his chest. The studded tires would make the sound of a zipper at that speed, the heater fan would putter against a crisp maple leaf that flipped wildly around inside the wire cage, and the woodrows in the pink light of sunup were like words he could just make out.

That was thirty years ago and Atticus was again on his way to the Denver airport, just a few weeks after he went there with Scott, and he recalled Scott looking out at the countryside and again reciting Gerard Manley Hopkins: " 'Birds build — but not I build; no, but strain, time's eunuch, and not breed one work that wakes. Mine, O thou lord of life, send my roots rain.' "

MEXICO

TWO

And it was Friday and Atticus was holding on to an overhead leather strap on a jolting second-class bus going east to Resurrección; too hot in his suit, his gray cowboy hat off, his lion-yellow overnight bag held between his legs as he squinted out through the gray smears of handprints and noses and sleeping heads on a rattling side window. Atticus was the only American among thirty Mexican passengers, many sitting with their dark eyes on him, the mothers patting babies who were swaddled in shawls, the grave brown men jouncing along in often-washed white shirts and straw cowboy hats, their fingers gripping the seat between their legs because of the high speed. A few feet from Atticus a fat driver of no more than twenty hung his belly over a wide steering wheel, hurtling the bus right and left by rolling the wheel with his elbows. A jeweled cross on a pink glass rosary was looped over the sun visor and was tapping against the spotted windshield. A four-color postcard of Pope John Paul II was taped next to the speedometer. Hot black oil was cooking on the hood, and the pandemonium in the engine was like iron pans being clapped together.

Off the highway a teenaged boy was walking into town with a sharp machete hooked onto his plastic belt, a .22 rifle slung over his right forearm, a giant pink and black iguana hanging by its tail. Lizards scattered into the weeds when the bus got closer than a few yards. Children stepped into deep weeds and raised their arms up for the gray and sultry wind that the blatting bus pulled along.

Wherever he looked the earth was orange and used up and no good for planting, but the trees were high as the sides of a canyon, the green turning to a night shade only twenty yards in. Some palm-thatched huts with sapling walls were at the fore edge of the forest, like outposts in a wilderness; deeper back there appeared to be little more than swamp and tangles and snarls of a seaweed moss that hung to the jungle floor like green strings of drying hair.

Iron gear teeth chattered together and caught as the fat man shifted to second and then hit the brake pedal too hard, tilting Atticus forward in the high whine of worn shoes on the brake drum. Hulking across the highway was an old Chevrolet pickup truck, its tail slung low with the heavy weight of a high concrete cross that six men were trying to fit into a hole for a roadside monument. Shouting was going on. Atticus crouched to peer at the cross through the front windshield and saw the hammered lettering for "Carmen Martínez." She was killed less than a week ago. She was sixteen years old.

Atticus looked farther ahead and saw what seemed like fifty accident markers along that winding half mile of highway: generally high white wood or concrete crosses, but also saints of plastic or painted clay or simple pyramids assembled from stones as big and round as grapefruit. *Recklessness,* he thought. And he thought of his wife. *You can end a life so easy.*

The tail lifted abruptly on the truck when the heavy cross was tilted up, and the truck's driver howled happily as he peeled across the highway into weeds. The fat bus driver sighed as he jammed into first gear and took off again, forcing Atticus back a step.

A hawk soared overhead, disappearing as it crossed over the bus and then reappearing in a lower part of the light blue sky, one wing dipping to veer it right. In the forest a tiny boy was flicking stones at the jutting ribs of skinny, longhorn, zebu cattle in order to steer them into a pole corral. And then there was an open countryside of yellow savannah and cocoa brown earth to the east and a stripe of the deep blue Caribbean Sea on top of the prairie for just a glimpse before the jungle interrupted again and Atticus saw a highway sign featuring symbols for food, gas, and lodging, and underneath them was RESURRECCIÓN.

Atticus looked at his *Spanish for Travellers* and experimented with the sentence before saying, *"Por favor, pare en la próxima parada."* According to Berlitz it meant, "Please let me off at the next stop," but he only heard a Spanish slang that was beyond his understanding as the fat driver jiggled the gear shift from side to side before ramming it into high. Atticus got down into the stairwell and saw a huge garbage dump made gray and white with seagulls, then a concrete housing development that was like row upon row of cheap motel rooms. A sign announced a *zona turística* was one kilometer away; and there was a Pemex gasoline station, a supermarket, a beauty shop, a few budget hotels that were called *posadas,* another teal and aquamarine snapshot of the Caribbean, and then there was a CENTRO sign, a great plaza and pink cathedral, a white gazebo in a main square of shade trees, and the high walls of government buildings.

"Aquí," Atticus said. Here.

"Claro," the Mexican said, and bumped the bus up onto the curb before yanking the emergency brake and flapping open the stairwell doors. Atticus was embarrassed to see that all thirty passengers were behind him, he needn't have pressed about the *parada,* but he smiled and said, *"Gracias,"* and heard a *"De nada"* as he got

54

out with the others into the hot sunlight and onto a sidewalk only two feet wide. The grand avenue that was called El Camino was paved with gray-blue cobblestones, and far down it were shops painted in the simple colors of gumballs, that seemed to sell only trinkets and postcards and Kodak film. A few Americans were sitting in the garden that faced the Church of the Resurrection or were strolling along the shaded loggia of the higher-class, air-conditioned stores.

A lime green taxi with a white top parked behind the second-class bus and a taxi driver with a gold-capped eyetooth and green paisley shirt jumped out, speaking to Atticus in rapid Spanish before he was twenty feet away.

Atticus flattened a half sheet of paper he'd been keeping in his suitcoat pocket and said, *"¿Como se llega a esta dirección?"* How do I get to this address?

The taxi driver took the paper and pretended to read the handwriting and then held up one finger, meaning Atticus ought to stay put, before he hustled across to an American Express travel agency to get someone inside to interpret the note.

Atticus looked across the main square and for an instant caught sight of a pretty European or American woman in front of the Printers Inc bookstore, in a fine black scarf and flashing sunglasses that hid her eyes. Was it Renata? She had the lithe body of a swimmer and skin that was tanned a ginger brown, and she seemed about to walk his way when the taxi driver hurried across from the American Express office, agreeing to get Atticus to the house and grabbing hold of his overnight bag.

Atticus got into the taxi and found a framed license in the name of Panchito Ramirez as the man turned the ignition and said, *"Sesentainueve, Avenida del Mar."* And Atticus thought about *sesentainueve* being the year his fourth well became his biggest oil find yet and he figured that from then on his family would be safe.

Sixty-nine Avenida del Mar was south past high-priced seaside hotels and then up a hill as steep as a playground slide on a street that was made of round stones. The taxi bumped along in second gear to get up the rise and then stopped at a high white wall and a gate of painted black wrought-iron spikes. His gold eyetooth showed as Panchito grinned in the rearview mirror at his august passenger and said, *"Cotzibaha."*

"Cotzibaha," Atticus repeated. He wanted to find out what it meant, but he was too tired and only English would come to him. He handsomely overpaid the man and got out with his bag.

An old gardener was standing in the driveway with a green hose, and water glintingly sheeted down the asphalt in a bright herringbone. Each peaked roof on the house was thatched in light brown rooster palm, and on the terraces of pink stone were potted sprays of flowers. Sixteenth-century iron hinges were on the great oak door, and there was an iron grillwork over the tiny lookout that opened after Atticus rapped the claw knocker four or five times.

A pretty Mexican woman in her twenties peeked out and Atticus Cody gave his full name. She disappeared from behind the iron grillwork and opened up the great oak door, and Atticus sidestepped inside with his bag as she said in Spanish that she couldn't speak English. She seemed to want more of an explanation, so Atticus said, *"Yo soy el padre del señor Cody."*

"Sí, señor," she said and placed her palm against her heart, saying, *"Me llamo María. La criada."* The maid. María pointed upstairs and spoke in her language, and Atticus guessed he was supposed to follow her up. He could see a high-gloss kitchen of red-painted brick and a dining room with sliding glass doors that opened onto a vast pink terrace and pool. Indian rugs in pastel shades of beige and green and purple and blue covered the floor of the big living room, but the dining room was just a highly polished pink marble. Four walls held fashionable expressionist paintings of the kinds favored by businesses and brass-framed prints announcing exhibitions at the Solomon R. Guggenheim Museum and the

Museum of Modern Art. The wide camelbacked sofas and chairs were cream white, as were the walls and window draperies. The house's owners had made a coffee table by placing smoked glass on the pink *cantera* stonework that seemed to have once been cornices on a church.

Atticus followed María upstairs and around a corner past a feminine bedroom and on into a field gray room where Scott had lived only two days ago. Atticus could still smell his fancy cologne. A football was on an Art Deco dresser that matched the track-lighted bed and high armoire and vanities. On a high-tech desk were sketch pads, books of poetry, a European telephone, and an IBM typewriter. A flat-screen television and videocassette recorder were inside a black cabinet of tinted glass, and high racks of hardback books in alphabetical order took up all of one wall. María had folded Scott's gold running shorts and placed them nicely on top of his sandy running shoes on the dressing room floor. Under glass on rough brown paper was "Atticus at Sixty," Scott's actual-size Crayola drawing of him as a pious, upright, presidential man, five feet nine inches tall, weighing a slight one hundred fifty pounds, the great grandson of a skinny kid who rode west with the Pony Express. Atticus walked out onto the upstairs terrace where he looked out on the azure water churning up to the shore and far away to his left saw a frail, gray lady lean over a balcony at the Maya Hotel with a highball glass in both hands, in filmy green pajamas and a forest green bathrobe that was gently sustained behind her by the hot late-afternoon breeze. She was his age, he guessed; financially set, familiar with solitude, finding rest whenever she could.

María asked, *"¿Está bien?"*

Atticus turned. "Looks okay to me."

María stooped in the bathroom to pick up a loose slip of paper and pushed it into her apron pocket, and then she gave the Spanish for the bath and dressing rooms and television and Caribbean vista as she went out and then came back in with soap and charcoal gray towels that she plumped down by the typewriter. She made an eating motion and showed Atticus seven fingers as she spoke words that he presumed were telling him when supper would be.

"Siete," he said.

"Sí, señor."

"Muy bien," Atticus said, *"y muchas gracias."* And as she went out, he finally took off his suitcoat and tie and shirt and began unpacking, putting his few things right on top of his son's in the dresser. Atticus had just the one other white shirt left and it was fresh and starched and folded inside plastic from the cleaners, and he thought he'd save that one for the funeral. So he hunted through the walk-in closet and got one of his

son's fancy rayon shirts off its hanger and tried it on. But he was surprised to find the cuffs were a full inch off his wrists and it was tight enough in the chest that the fabric strained. Six shirts in the closet were like it, European and high-priced and a full size too small, a fourteen-inch neck and a thirty-inch sleeve; the others were Hathaway and Arrow and fitted him like his own. Atticus figured he'd ask María about it, but then he imagined himself fighting for the right words in Spanish as she frowned with worry, and so he forgot about it and just put on a fresh white Hathaway. He slid his overnight bag underneath the wide bed, and then he sat on it in order to look over the paperbacks that were next to a square water glass on the bedside table. Scott had been up to page 39 in *The Secret Sharer* by Joseph Conrad, and he'd been highlighting in yellow a book of writings from pre-Hispanic Mexico. Atticus went to the bookmark, but his sore eyes couldn't make out the book's print until he got his gold-rimmed spectacles out of their leather pocket case and hooked them on over his ears. A highlighted paragraph read:

There is no place of well-being on the earth, there is no happiness, no pleasure. They say that the earth is the place of painful pleasure, of grievous happiness. The elders have always said: "So that we should not go round always moaning, that we should not be filled with sadness, the Lord has given us laughter, sleep, food, our strength and fortitude, and finally the act by which we propagate." All this sweetens life on earth so that we are not always moaning. But even though it be like this, even though it be true that there is only suffering and this is the way things are on earth, even so, should we always be afraid? Should we always be fearful? Must we live weeping? But see there is life on the earth, there are the lords; there is authority, there is nobility, there are eagles and tigers. And who is always saying that so it is on earth? Who goes about trying to put an end to his life? There is ambition, there is struggle, work. One looks for a wife, one looks for a husband.

Atticus thought, *Wife;* he thought, *Husband. Who goes about trying to kill himself?* The bookmark was a Mexican, gold-leafed card with a bright but ugly painting on the front. The handwriting inside said:

Dear Scott,
I hope you're feeling some better. I really can't tell you how sorry I am for your unhappiness and frustration. Circumstances have not been kind. You have a life to get on

with, and I have a difficult relationship to figure out — both daunting enterprises. And it seems for the time being that neither of us is in a position to help the other with his or her respective task. Too many tangled feelings . . .

When you do feel truly comfortable with a friendship — for that is all I can offer — I hope you will call or write me. Your friendship means more to me than it seems you realize.

Try to be good to yourself.
I love you,

Renata

Atticus shut the card inside the book and walked down the hallway to the feminine guest bedroom with its face lotions and face powders arrayed on a dresser. He looked into the walk-in closet, finding four or five blouses, some folded blue jeans, a few skirts and dresses, a jumble of shoes, and a hard-sided green suitcase shut tight with a red shock cord. On the handle an old, dog-eared luggage claim check from Mexicana Airlines indicated a flight from Miami to Cancún. Hoisting a bed pillow, he folded back the pink and lavender comforter and saw there were no sheets on the mattress underneath.

Atticus found Scott's United States passport and Mexican visa mislaid on a bookshelf and carried them back with him to his suitcase, fitting them in a side pocket with his socks. Then he just looked at the field gray bedroom's furnishings for a while, trying to find a fraction of Scott in them and failing.

He focused on the desk and pulled out the upper right-hand drawer, seeing pastel-colored pencils and pens in a plastic tray, gum erasers, pen tips, inks, knives that were like fierce hospital scalpels. Everything was just as it was in his desk at home. Atticus wondered if the kitchen dishware would be to the right of the sink and the Cheer on the floor by the washer. In the second drawer were Mexican stamps and brown envelopes and letterhead writing paper and an old green address book that would have fallen apart without Scotch tape. Looking under *C,* he saw "Frank and Marilyn Cody," with their mailing address and telephone number. And below that was "Atticus and Serena Cody," as though they were just cousins or good neighbors whom Scott sent holiday cards to. Atticus flipped through other pages and was aggrieved by all the names he couldn't recognize. Every now and then he'd come upon a high school coach still in Antelope, a Stanford art history professor whom Scott had talked about, a California girlfriend, or a painter Scott had introduced his father to at one of his East Village parties, but for the most part the address book was crowded with foreign people

63

Atticus had never heard of, with geography he had never been in; it might have been the address book of an acquaintance or even a man Atticus had never known but who had, by chance, known him.

Atticus said aloud, "Who are you?" and then put away the address book and left the upstairs room for the first-floor terrace and the tiers of railroad ties that formed a stairway down to the seashore. Atticus looked to his left boot and watched a hermit crab scutter away from him and work sideways into a hole. A black pinhead of an eye stared up at Atticus for a second, and then its big claw slashed wildly at the hole's entrance and in the fall of sand the hermit crab buried itself underground.

Scott, he thought. Hiding things from him ever since he was a kid. Atticus walked up to the terrace and there he achingly got into a white chaise lounge and knitted his fingers atop his gray hair, just lying there in the chilling sea breeze and the hurrying darkness, hearing María in the kitchen, trying not to think of anything, but thinking and thinking about his son.

María served him a tostada salad without peppers or hot sauce, then worked speedily in the kitchen, putting some wash in the Maytag clothes dryer and getting her apron off as soon as she'd cleared his plate. She seemed eager to be gone from the house. She stopped by the dining room and said without pleasure, *"Buenas noches, señor."*

The only phrase Atticus could immediately recall was, *"Hasta mañana."*

María shook her head and said, *"Hasta el lunes,"* and then pointed down to the floor, saying, *"Aquí, el lunes."* She could see Atticus wasn't comprehending, so she attempted some English. *"He-yer moonday,"* she said.

"Are you getting paid for this?"

She looked at him in puzzlement.

Atticus tried, *"¿Tiene usted dinero?"*

María said haltingly, "Escott he is pay me *hasta marzo.*"

"Until March."

"Sí, señor."

Atticus acknowledged that with a thumb-up and María went out, and he stayed in his dining room chair as night gained in the rooms. A regular tinking, scritching noise from the Maytag dryer was finally irritating enough that he got up and fished his hand around in the hot air and still-damp clothes until he found a Schlage key on a red plastic tag with the number 13 stamped into it. Having no idea where Scott kept his keys, he started up the dryer again, pulled an upper drawer in the kitchen counter where batteries rolled up against hand tools and torn newspaper coupons, and he tossed the key in there. *You're getting fussy in your old age,* he thought, and he found his *Spanish for Travellers* and studied it at the dining room table until the book wore him out. He kept thinking he ought to phone Renata or that American consul, or go so far as to get in touch with the Mexican police, but his engines were running down and it was good to just sit there hearing fiesta music from the hotel and under that the night sea growling onto the shore like feed grain falling into a cattle trough. Winter in Colorado, the horses in their stalls, and Scott flat on the floor half a lifetime ago, watching in awe, his chin on his hands, as his older brother glued together racing cars.

And then Atticus woke up to the ringing of the telephone and was surprised to find he'd been sleeping. He got up stiffly from the dining room chair and located the phone, but when he picked up the receiver and said "Hello," he quailed at hearing Scott's prerecorded voice: "Hi. You know the routine, name and number. I'll get back atcha later." Atticus hung there, shakily waiting to hear the offered message, but whoever was first on the phone was now off. And yet the green light on the answering machine beside the phone was blinking twice, meaning, he supposed, that there were two earlier messages.

Atticus pushed the rewind button, heard the reels spin to a halt, and pushed playback, his face changing like a page of a book slowly turned as he heard a soft, foreign, male voice saying, "*Hola,* Scott. Are you at the fiesta with Renata? Have a fantastic time. I hate plays, plus in addition I have laundry to do. Don't worry, I have my own key. Shall we meet at the Bancomex at ten tomorrow?"

Right after that was a tone, and then Renata's voice saying, "Hey? If you're still around, we're having a cast party at Stuart's. Wanna come? See ya."

Wednesday night. Atticus was going to press rewind but then thought he ought to preserve the voices; he wasn't sure why. His neck was sore and his right arm tingled. He went into the high-gloss red kitchen and opened an icebox bottle of *agua mineral.* He kept hearing the European voice: fontosstic for fantastic, haff for have; stressing each syllable like he was hitting a snake with a stick. María had hung up her apron on a hook over a mop and dustpan and broom of green straw. Atticus slipped his fingers into the apron pocket and pulled out the two-by-three-inch piece of paper that she'd picked up from the bathroom floor upstairs. It was simply a Monday sales receipt from a *farmacia* on Calle Hidalgo. He couldn't tell what kind of medicine it was for, and for some reason he thought he ought to. The pesos worked out to forty dollars. Atticus folded up the receipt and put it in his wallet.

And he found in a catchall basket on the

kitchen countertop a Kodak snapshot of Renata and Scott and half a dozen happy people he never knew at some kind of grand affair in the dining room, food filling the table, fifty wineglasses it looked like, green champagne bottles chilling in an ice chest under the dining room table. Cold water from it was oozing darkly onto the broad pink and blue Indian rug. He lifted his frown from the photograph and looked to the dining room floor. The Indian rug was no longer there. Under the party snapshot was another, of salt white sand and a high sun kindling the azure sea, an old red Volkswagen wallowing into its tire ruts, one door wide as if an interior radio were playing. Twenty feet away from the camera, Scott was nakedly crouched in his architecture of a great sandcastle, its turrets constructed of uncorked bottles that once contained burgundy wine. And Renata Isaacs was lying just to his left, inviting the sun to her naked body, one forearm slung over her eyes, her gorgeous breasts unhidden, her ginger brown thighs tilted up so that fine white sand powdered the undersides and the faint hint of her sex.

Atticus shut his eyes and tried to slaughter his thoughts, but they hung with him as he put the snapshots in the basket, got another *agua mineral,* and held the cold green bottle in his hand.

She came over at nine. Atticus heard a Volkswagen engine haul up and got to the front door in his pajamas and slippers just as Renata knocked on it. She looked embarrassed over getting him up. His eyes were very red and his gray white hair was jackstrawed until his hand combed it down. Dogs were barking up and down the avenue and Renata Isaacs was standing uncertainly on the brick sidewalk in skin-tight blue jeans and an Irish sweater that she'd pushed up on her arms. She called him by his first name, and then she shrieked with hurt and misery and flung herself into him with the freedom of a wife. She cried for four or five minutes and Atticus petted her hair and just held her. With carefulness.

She finally pulled her face away from him and wiped her hazy eyes with her wrist. She smiled with shame. "I was trying not to do that."

Atticus said, "Don't you give it a thought," and invited her inside. And then he went upstairs to get into his green tartan robe.

She was hunting knowingly through the sideboard in the dining room when he got back downstairs. She found a box of matches and held a flame to the candles. She asked, "Don't you hate overhead lighting?"

Atticus didn't say. She looked up at him as she waved out the match and put it back inside the matchbox. She said, "Ever since yesterday I've been looking for things to complain about."

"And nothing's wrong enough."

Renata dimmed the dining room lights with the

rheostat and smiled. "At least it's good to see you again."

"You too."

She pulled out a dining room chair as though she always sat in that one place. Atticus sat across from her.

She was not as beautiful as she'd been when he'd first met her fourteen years ago. She seemed tired and afflicted, there were hints of wrinkles and crow's feet, and there was plenty of gray in the sable brown hair that was long and fashionably unruly. But Renata still had the face of a forties actress, a face to fall in love with, like Vivien Leigh, he thought, like Gene Tierney. Sitting in the dining room chair with her hands and elbows and breasts on the table and a flashing look of agreement in her tobacco-brown eyes, Renata seemed as affectionate as a favorite daughter, and he found himself grinning with fatherly foolishness as he said, "Good to see you."

Renata said, "You too. We keep saying that."

"How are you holding up?"

"Fine."

"You sleeping okay?"

"Eh." She attempted a smile. "I hoped you'd come down. I kept trying to phone you yesterday, to say you ought to, but your line was always busy."

"Talking to friends."

She propped her cheek on one hand and tapped a blue candlestick, making the golden flame tremble and then attain its height again.

"Was that you at the bookstore this afternoon?"

Renata blanked her face.

"Wasn't sure if it was you or not. You had sunglasses on."

"Oh, I'm sorry. I had a lot on my mind."

"I kind of figured."

"You got here okay, though?"

"Well, they're good people here; they help out as much as they can."

"Are you taking it okay?"

"Don't know what *okay* is. I'm sad. I'm lonesome for him. I'm angry with him for doing it, and angrier with myself for not being able to stop it." Atticus thought and then he imagined blood on his son and he wiped his eyes with the heel of his palm. He forced his lips together to keep them still.

Renata said, "I cried myself out."

Atticus sighed. "You get used to these things. But they still twist you up pretty tight."

"I know."

"You ever consider having children, Renata?"

She shook her head.

"I meant in the future."

"I understood."

"Children give you a second chance to get

71

things right. You grow up all over again. But you're so dang responsible. We worried all the time about our boys. Even the thought of my kids catching colds used to get me half frenzied."

"Scott loved you very much," Renata said.

"Well, I thought the world of him. Hope he knew that." Atticus brought the right side of his robe over his pajama top, gathering it tight again. "I hate the idea of it being hasty. You'd like to think he gave it some thought at least."

She seemed tuned out for a moment, as if hearing a hushed conversation in another room. And then she said, "Lately I haven't been privy to his thoughts. We've been apart a lot."

"You slept here off and on, though, didn't you? With Scott?"

She hesitated before she admitted, "We had an arrangement."

"Stuart and you."

She hesitated again, then nodded.

"Your clothes here is how I knew. And no sheets on the other bed."

"It wasn't just me. Scott partied a lot."

"Partied," Atticus said.

She seemed about to give him examples but thought better of it. "We all live on the fringe here. We make up the rules as we go along."

Atticus scowled at the orchids upright in a vase on the sideboard. Sink water had greened to the color of vinegar. "Scott gave me the impression you were getting back together."

She sighed. "Oh, I don't know. We were still cordial. But all the intensity was on his part. I'm really trying to get it right with Stuart."

Atticus stared at Renata without comment, and she shied away from it. She looked at the kitchen. After a while he said, "Taxi driver seemed to know this house. Called it Cozy-something."

"*Cotzibaha.* It's a Mayan honorific for 'house of the artist.' "

"Was Scott that famous?"

"He went native when he first got here. Hung out with a shaman named Eduardo. And he gave them money. You get famous fast doing that."

"I suppose." Atticus looked at the hard calluses of his hands and scratched at one with his thumbnail. "Another thing. Was he joking or was Scott truly renting this house from criminals?"

She laughed. "Marty? Marty sells real estate in Chicago."

"Oh. I get it."

"You asked that like a detective."

"Well . . ." He held a hand against his yawn. "Would you like some coffee, or, I don't know, a pop?"

"Yes, I think so." Atticus half-lifted from his chair, but she was already up. "Don't. I'll get it."

She got a Corona from the refrigerator and was rummaging for an opener in a kitchen drawer when she caught sight of the Kodak snapshots.

73

She glanced at him and found knowledge of her in his face. She worriedly stared at her shameless pose on the sand, then flipped the pictures into the basket and blushed with embarrassment as she sat with him again. She drank beer straight from the bottle and finished half before she placed it in front of her.

"Stuart take it?"

"We weren't a ménage à trois, if that's what you're asking."

Atticus softly petted his hair. "I'm finding my education kinda deficient here."

She smiled. "We weren't a threesome."

"Oh." Atticus reddened and said, "You got my mind reeling now."

"It shows."

"Those pictures. I was just hunting anything handy. You know, to try to figure things out."

She was all inwardness for a while, and she faced nothing as she said, "Unfortunately there's not much to know."

She told him she'd first seen Scott on Wednesday afternoon. She was just coming from a friend's studio at the American College where she'd been sitting as a nude model. "We needed the money," she said.

"We?"

"Well, just me, I guess. Wrong pronoun."

"You'll inherit twenty-five thousand from his trust fund. Frank had a look at his will."

"*Really?* How sweet of him." She gave it some thought and then changed her expression. She ran a hand through her hair. "Shall I go on?"

She told him she walked with Scott to The Scorpion at five and Stuart joined them a half hour later. Scott hardly talked to her or Stuart, and he drank like drunkenness was the whole idea. Wednesday was a fiesta and there was a Children's Defense Fund benefit at a hall in the Marriott, where they paid twenty dollars each for Mexican food on paper plates and Renata and four other Americans gave a reading of Tennessee Williams's *The Night of the Iguana.* She once looked up from a page of the script and saw Scott sitting far in the back and holding a full pitcher of margarita up to his mouth like a frat boy, and she got so angry she hardly spoke to him afterward. And then he disappeared and she threw a cast party at Stuart's villa and she regretted her anger and tried to telephone him at his house. There was no answer, so she left a message. Late that night Scott telephoned her and said he'd forgotten where he'd parked his Volkswagen but he was pretty sure it was in the *jardín.* Would she get it for him? Scott told her he was finishing up something at the house in the jungle where he painted.

"And how'd he sound?"

"Distracted and harried and really tired," she said. "I offered to go out there, because it sounded like he could use a friend, but he was

75

pretty insistent that he have a few days on his own." Renata's eyes welled with tears. "I hear that conversation over and over again, and there's nothing in his voice that would have made me think he was going to do what he did."

Atticus was sitting there, listening intently, his hard blue eyes fixed on his crossed and hairless white ankles, as still as if he were cut out of ice. "But you went out there. Even though he said not to."

Renata said she was opening Stuart's bookstore the first thing in the morning because Stuart had to go see their wholesaler. She got down to the *jardín* around sunrise and too easily found Scott's car. Even if he were drunk he ought to have drifted across it. She thought something was wrong. So she forgot about the bookstore and went out there. She glimpsed a shotgun on the floor and Scott sitting in a green leather wingback chair. His face had been half shot off.

"How long had he been dead?"

"We don't know."

"Was there a note or anything?"

"Signed on his sketch pad. 'No one is to blame.' "

Atticus heard it, and heard it again. "Well, heck, I feel better already. How about you? *Huh?* We're both off the hook."

She reached a hand toward him. "He wasn't thinking."

Weighed low with grief, all Atticus could manage was, "We didn't raise him to —" And then he fell silent and held a hand to his eyes and cried.

Renata got up from the dining room table and walked around it in order to wrap her arms around him and press her hot cheek against his hair. "We've been put through a lot," she said.

Atticus held himself stiffly, then finally patted her left hand and said, "You ought to go now. It's late."

"If it's okay, I'll stay here."

"I'd like that."

She stood up from him but petted her hand on his hard shoulder as she said, "The funeral Mass is at noon. You'll have to bury him in Mexico for now."

"I'll want to get him up to our family plot in Antelope."

"You probably can, but it will take a little time. Stuart can help you with the government people you'll have to pay off. You can bribe your way out of practically anything here. *La mordida,* they call it: the bite."

Atticus stared out at the moonshine on the sea. And then he asked, "How about the police? Was there a police report or, you know, an investigation?"

"Don't expect much from it," Renata said. "The Mexican police don't get too involved in

American cases unless our government instructs them to do otherwise. Which they're not likely to do. And there's no coroner; no autopsy; probably just a pro forma investigation. Mexico can be pretty casual about suicide."

"Suicide," Atticus said, and spoke no more. When he looked up again, he realized Renata had already gone upstairs.

Much later Atticus woke to words composed with the ticking *k*'s and *t*'s of Mayan speech. Getting into his green tartan robe and slippers, he walked down the steps until he could stoop and look into the candlelighted dining room. Four *campesinos* in white shirts and white pants were familiarly slapping poker cards onto the dining table and sipping Jameson's Irish whiskey from a green bottle that was being passed around. A fat man was using a nailhead to scrape tobacco out of his pipe bowl into a frail teacup while another man played a jack of hearts by pounding it down with his hand. A little man in his forties with flowing hair and a Padres baseball cap turned around in his dining room chair and solemnly peered at him, and Atticus tramped back upstairs.

Lights were on in Renata's room and the door was halfway open. Even in high school, these were the hours Scott furiously painted, his stereo faintly playing Edith Piaf or early Bob Dylan, the hallway full of the pungence of turpentine and Marlboro cigarettes. Atticus knocked softly and heard Renata ask, *"¿Quién es?"* Who is it?

"Me," he said.

"You too, huh?"

He found her sitting up in bed in a far-too-open pink kimono, a book of Shakespeare's plays held against her stomach. A half-full Corona was in her left hand. Atticus forced himself to turn his head away, and Renata tightened her robe. She asked, "You look in on his friends?"

"Had a peek. Which one was Eduardo?"

She was surprised. "You've got a good memory. The guy in the Padres cap, I think." She took a mouthful of beer and chilled her neck with the bottle. "Scott would go out to their shacks in the *barrio,* feed on their fried dog meat and iguanas, get horribly sick with their sicknesses, and then go out there again with their next invitation. He said they made him an honorary Mayan." She smiled. "You don't suppose it's possible that it was all sarcasm on their part, do you?"

"Well, he always was a friendly kid."

She fell into a reverie as she said, "And he'd try just about anything."

"What is it downstairs, some kind of a wake?"

"I hear they pretend a friend has played a good trick on the world and they party like they're in on the joke." She drank some beer and held the bottle on the mattress. "Their funerals take place a year later when they rebury the body. And then they howl with sadness."

Atticus looked at a clock by her bed. After two. "Well, morning comes awful early," he said.

"You know what the name Atticus means? Scott told me. Simplicity, purity, and intelligence."

"Always making things up, that kid."

"You two are so interesting. You're the formidable figure he idolized and struggled not to become, and he's who you'd be if you didn't have all your good habits and rules and boundaries."

"I forgot. You studied psychology."

Renata flushed and put a hand to her face. "I just realized: I was using the present tense."

"Hard not to," he said.

She focused on him and then on her book. "Shall I read to you?" She took his silence as permission, and she beautifully read from Shakespeare's *King John*: " 'Grief fills the room up of my absent child, lies in his bed, walks up and down with me, puts on his pretty looks, repeats his words, remembers me of all his gracious parts, stuffs out his vacant garments with his form.' " Renata closed the book and her brown eyes sorrowed as she recited, " 'Then have I reason to be fond of Grief.' "

THREE

Atticus walked out to the pool in his pajamas with hot coffee in a cup. The terra-cotta tiles were cool against his feet, but the salt air was as warm as it is in a parlor of tall windows. A gray freighter was just in sight, forcing its way so slowly it seemed stopped, and a fishing boat with Americans in sunglasses on board was angling out into the Gulf Stream. Along the salt white beaches, Mexican boys in hotel jackets were kicking out deck chairs and cranking open big umbrellas and putting out the red plastic flags that warned of the undertow with the word *peligroso*. A swallow flew across the yard and alighted on an upstairs railing. The swallow cocked its head to the right, jabbed a half-smoked cigarette out of an ashtray up there, and then flew away. The cigarette stirred in the wind and rolled along the railing. The frame of the tall sliding glass door between the dining room and the terrace was harshly scratched and indented near its lock as if a pike or a crowbar had forced it open. Either it was thieves, he guessed, or like as not his son forgot his front door keys.

Water was on in a shower upstairs. Atticus finished his coffee and went back inside and turned on the gas burner under the glass coffee-pot. Whispers and dish noise had awakened him at sunup as the Mayans tidied the place when their wake was over. One of them had put the Jameson's whiskey bottle on the red kitchen windowsill. Oranges were in a pink string bag by the refrigerator; copper pans were hanging over the stove. Atticus opened a side cupboard and found it jammed with bottles of spice and vitamins and a plastic bag of chopped green weed, presumably marijuana. Atticus sighed and put a slice of Wonder bread in the toaster. Wires in the toaster glowed orange as he looked out through the sink window's wooden louvers to an old red Volkswagen that hadn't been there yesterday. Sketch pads and paints and rolled-up canvases overheaped the seats. His toast popped up and he spooned on jam, thinking, *You'll have to get an inventory.* His coffee boiled and he turned off the gas burner. He refilled his cup and sipped from it as he wandered into the dining room. A shotgun shell of a brass lipstick case was standing upright on the sideboard. Hadn't been there before. Mayans probably found it on the floor when they cleaned up. Atticus took off the top and saw that its blood-red tip was crumbled, and then he saw a faint trace of red on the dining room mirror he was facing.

A freshly showered Renata skipped down the steps in her pink kimono, her hair tangling wetly at her collar. "Aren't those pajamas smart," she said, and slipped past him to get four oranges out of the string bag in the kitchen and a paring knife out of a wooden block by the stove.

"I was fishing for compliments," Atticus said.

"Sleep well?" she asked, but sought no answer. Sleeplessness welted her own eyes, and she seemed petulant and irritated. She halved the oranges and placed them in a juicer, then pulled the juicer's handle down harder than the oranges demanded.

She wiped a juice glass against the pink silk. "How about some o.j.?"

"Had some."

Renata drank juice from her glass and slapped the paring knife into the wooden block. "Weird day," she said. Her voice harbored the hushed abrasion of a shoe on carpet.

His hand wiped a trickle from the hot-water faucet handle. Bad washer. "Looked upstairs for his wallet," he said. "Expect the police have it still."

"Don't know."

"I found this lipstick."

She looked at it. "Oh, thanks." She put it in her kimono pocket.

"Wasn't my color."

She faintly smiled. "You're more a Spring, aren't you."

"Well, I try to be."

Silence hung in the air between them like cigarette smoke.

Atticus finally asked, "Was there a break-in here? Door there looked jimmied open."

She fell into thought and then she offered, "Either that or he lost his keys. Drunks do lose things."

"Was he that way often?"

She lifted her glass. "Maybe just around me."

"And why's that?"

She finished her orange juice before saying, "I hate this."

"Hate what?"

She put her hands flat on the kitchen counter-top and paused as if rehearsing what she was about to say. But the front door opened and a high male voice called, *"¡Hola!"* Renata informed Atticus secretly, as if cheating, "Stuart," and then called back, "In the kitchen!"

Stuart Chandler was a tall, fashionable Englishman of Atticus's age, with a full head of white hair he'd sleeked back with gel, skin that was a mahogany brown, and shrewd, impatient, hazel green eyes. Dressed in a fine black blazer but pleated white trousers and white docksiders, he seemed a yachtsman, and he sauntered into the kitchen as if he wanted to talk to the chef, first smiling at Renata, then firmly shaking Atticus's hand and offering his name in the way of a famous man often introduced. Stuart said, "I only wish we could be meeting in happier circumstances, Mr. Cody. I have three grown sons of my own, so I think I can fathom the feelings you must have now. You do have my deepest sympathy."

"Appreciate it," he said.

"Are you coping?"

"Oh yeah." Atticus filled his cup. "How about some coffee?"

"No, thank you. Cigarettes are my only poison." He looked affectionately at Renata. "And how are you, darling?"

Renata said she was fine. She put her orange-juice glass in the sink.

Atticus paused and said, "Renata was telling me last night you could help get my boy's body out of Mexico."

"Yes," Stuart said, "but there's a ludicrous bureaucracy to battle first. We'll have to bury Scott today and hope for intercession from the United States Embassy in Mexico City. I have position but no power, alas. And we need permission to have him exhumed. I heard from . . . Frank?"

"Frank," he said.

"We talked about it just this morning. Our thinking is harmonious. You can go home to Colorado tonight, and I'll be pleased to assume the burden of having him shipped up to Ante-lope."

"I'll do it. You don't have to *pop* for me to ship my own boy."

Stuart turned to Renata. "Oh, was that patron-izing?"

"Stuart meant —"

"Forget it," Atticus said.

Stuart held his gaze on him. "We are expected at the funeral parlor," he said. And with the frankness of someone used to having his orders obeyed, Stuart added, "Hadn't you better go get changed?"

And he was sitting on the right of an air-con-ditioned Dodge station wagon as Stuart Chandler gingerly urged it along a street that was rough as an alley. Atticus had gotten into a white shirt that was as hard as cardboard, a gray silk tie, a fancy black cashmere suit that would be too hot by noontime, and his highly polished lizard-skin boots. Stuart had rolled down his side window four inches so he could hold his Salem cigarette far from offense, and he faced away from Atticus when he exhaled. Atticus had run out of things to say. He held his gray cowboy hat in one hand and flattened his hair and the gray wings of his mus-tache as he looked out at the *centro*.

Green and pink buildings were high above them on both sides and hot sunlight glared like snow off the walls. Dark old women were sitting in the shade of doorways and saying things to famished children. Skinny dogs were running at the station wagon's tires and jumping up at the side windows as Atticus scowled down.

"Atticus," Stuart said. "Wasn't that the name —"

"Yes."

"Of the father in —"

"To Kill a Mockingbird."

"You've had this conversation before."

"Up until the sixties I had the name to myself."

"I shall bathe you in silence," Stuart said. He turned the car onto El Camino Real and was forced to stop for a friendly man pushing a *frijoles* cart. Stuart let the Salem fall from his hand into the street. He drove forward. "I have been a citizen of the United States since 1962," he said. "I first went there to be the pre-Columbian art specialist at Sotheby's. Have you heard of Sotheby's, Mr. Cody?"

"Auction house."

"Well, I got sacked, to put it frankly, and it was the best thing that ever happened to me. A friend asked, as I was unemployed, if I was interested in taking over his little Mexican shop, selling paperback books in English. And I fell quite in love with the place." Stuart seemed to grow bored with the thought. Half a minute later he said, "What a bother love is."

An unhappy girl in a dirty pink dress was wrapping hot corn tortillas in sheets of newspaper outside a shop. A frail old man was carrying kindling up the hill in a sling that was looped over his forehead.

Stuart fought to have a conversation and said, "I have been the American consul here for five years now." A havoc of lines hatched his roasted brown face.

"A pretty good job, is it?"

"Well, it isn't a job so much as a social position. And there's no pay, of course, and that is a pity."

"You oughta be real proud."

"Don't encourage me. We had a police chief here, the *jefe;* he's retired now, but you know where he was from? Omaha! The town has gone to hell since he left. Omaha's near Denver, isn't it?"

"Eight hours by car if you speed."

"Oh, *facts,*" he said. Stuart stared ahead. "The chamber of commerce here has fourteen members whose origins are Europe or Canada or the United States, compared to just thirty Mexicans. If you go to hospital, you'll find no less than one-fourth of the doctors and nurses have their degrees from the U.S. And the current principal of the high school is from Williams College, in Massachusetts. We are like the Romans in Palestine, the British in India. We are less than ten percent of the population but provide seventy-two percent of its tax base. And so we are catered to." Stuart peered farther down the street and said, "Hup!" and braked, further rolling down his side window as he said, "My beggar."

A one-legged man on crutches swung along on his good leg to get to the car. His iron gray eyes looked in at Atticus and then at Stuart and then he hung his hand out on the rolled-down window glass. Stuart talked to him in Spanish, held out a half-dollar in peso notes, and then rolled up the window again. The one-legged man was crossing himself and speaking Spanish as Stuart drove away.

"Hector prays for me. Words very pretty to the ear, a poem about my charity being recorded in Heaven. All very stupid, of course, but in a poor country one is expected to pay a little to the street people, and I have chosen Hector." Stuart rapped the horn and a boy scampered off the road. The boy watched them pass with a soccer ball on his hip. Stuart smiled. "You see how my Hector was looking for me? Already this morning he has probably stopped by my villa. Such fidelity! I hope to finally elope with Hector. We'll float on bright rafts in the Bay of Campeche."

Stuart went down Cinco de Mayo street and then into a greenly shaded alley. He stopped the car in a dirt parking area behind a pink mortuary that was called Cipiano. Stuart paused as he opened his door. "Are you prepared for this, Atticus?"

"Have to be."

Stuart got out but then angled under the station wagon's ceiling. "You could wait in the car, perhaps. Or you could go over to the *parroquia.* Renata will be there soon."

Atticus got out of the Dodge and nudged the door closed. "You go ahead and I'll be at your heels."

The pink mortuary's interior was as cool and damp as a flower shop. A plump woman in a green shift that she'd hiked up high on her thighs was squirting a floor with hose water, and four shy brown men in straw cowboy hats and snap-buttoned polyester shirts were standing apart from a painted black coffin that looked more like a hope chest. Hewn into its soft pine wood were rising suns, pheasants, butterflies, and flowers. Tilted atop the coffin was a copper-framed pic-ture of a fiery Sacred Heart of Jesus held within a green crown of thorns. A heavy man in a gray sharkskin suit and heavily pomaded, wavy hair slid a purple kneeler across the room, halted it at the head of the coffin, and held his hand on it as he hinted the father of the deceased forward.

Atticus dipped off his cowboy hat and got down onto the kneeler with pain. His hand floated over wood that was still tacky with paint as he offered up the familiar prayers he'd been saying since he was a child. Without turning, he asked the Englishman, "Would they open it?" He heard Stuart's fluent Spanish and faced him. The guy in the sharkskin suit was up on his toes, whispering into Stuart's ear.

"Cipiano is saying you are not permitted inspection," Stuart said. "Embalming isn't done here, you see." He waited for another sentence. "And it has been already two days."

Atticus heard a phrase from holy Scripture, *Lord, by this time he stinketh.* He looked around for a hand tool and a hunched, old Mexican found a claw hammer for him to pull the finishing nails from the top with, but when he took it from him Atticus felt his back so softly touched by another he hardly knew the owner was there. And he stared up at Cipiano as he held his hands in prayer at his chin, his face a wreck of sorrow. *"Está feo, Señor Cody,"* he said, and Stuart translated, "He is ugly."

"Le falta la cara."

"The face is missing."

"Hicimos todo lo posible."

"His people did what they could."

"Es mejor recordar su hijo que verlo."

"Cipiano says it is better to remember your son than to see him."

Atticus held the hammer and knelt there, thinking how he'd feel if he did what it was better to have done. And he fought against Cipiano's wishes and used the hammer to pry up ten finishing nails and tilt up the coffin lid.

But it was too awful; he gave it just a few seconds. A hot blast of horrible stink forced him back with a hand over his nose and mouth, and he only had a quick, hideous glimpse of Scott before he let the coffin lid fall: his blond hair in chaos, his teeth gray and clenched as if he were biting hard on a stick, and half his face just a stew of skin and bone, the other half green with huge swelling.

Atticus stood there, his hands at his sides, as the funeral parlor's carpenters nailed down the pine again, and then he helped the Mexicans hoist the painted coffin and ferry it out to the station wagon and slide it into the open rear. The old Dodge was so low-slung with the heavy weight that iron rang off the cobbled paving when Cipiano gently eased the car toward Cinco de Mayo. And then Stuart and Atticus strolled the four blocks to the parish church, Atticus keeping his hands in his pockets and his pink face tilted up to the sun. They had fifteen minutes until the funeral. Stuart fought a wink as he said, "Isn't *Renata* the sultry number."

"She's a lovely woman."

"Oh, none of that! She's a *siren!*"

Atticus shot him a fierce glance and said, "I got other things on my mind."

"I have offended your courtliness, haven't I."

Atticus failed to reply.

Stuart's face changed and they walked in silence for a few minutes. And he asked, "How old are you, Atticus?"

"Sixty-seven."

"I shall be sixty-four in May. And I fear I shan't be much older." Stuart stopped by the party-colored cart of a man selling paper cones of green ice and asked, "Will you permit me?"

"Okay."

Stuart held up two fingers, saying *"Dos,"* and passed one cone to him. The green was peppermint and the ice was a nice pain to his teeth, but only after he'd chewed up the greater part of it did he wonder if the ice water was pure. Stuart sipped at his and tipped his nose toward a pink church that was trumped up with European lacework and Gothic belfries and spires. "Such fraudulence," he said. *"La parroquia.* Architectural gumbo."

A five- or six-year-old boy offered to polish his shoes, but Stuart stepped aside and said, *"No, no me gusta."* The hurt boy looked at Atticus, but he shook his head.

Stuart said, "Renata hates Cipiano; he finds too many reasons to touch her. Not that I blame him." He looked at the *jardín* just across from the church. Wide laurel trees shaded the sidewalks, and green flower beds circled the great white gazebo in the center. Young teenaged girls

93

in the kinds of white dresses one sees at First Communions were strolling in groups of four or five while boys hunting *novias* hung back and talked about them. Stuart asked, "Are you in love, Atticus?"

"Was. With my wife. And I got grandkids now."

"But it's not the same, is it." Hearing nothing from him, he said, "I have often wished I weren't in love. I often find the feeling indistinguishable from hurt."

Stuart looked up at the parish church and said, "You go ahead, all right? I *have* to have a cigarette."

Atticus walked past him, sidestepping between halted cars and carts and crossing over to the great plaza in front of the church. A hospital clinic had been set up inside the old rectory. Crowding outside it were pregnant women, a dark man with a goiter in his neck like a plum, a girl with a cotton patch over her mouth, and a stump of a man with toes that were only partly covered by a rolled-up and bloody sock. On the steps of the Church of the Resurrection was a hunched woman so wrapped in a blue serape that she was no more than a nose and an open hand, and in the dark pews inside were more old women with rosaries, harshly whispering their prayers. Campesinos were stacking unshucked corn on a linen altar cloth below a statue of Saint Martin de

Porres, and tacked up over a side altar were tin cards with childlike illustrations of fractured bones or maladies or crippled people in sickbeds. Words on the tin cards either sought the saint's help or gave thanks for the cure that came. Up near the main altar the Mexican pallbearers were setting the painted coffin down in the Saint Joseph side chapel as a handsome Mexican priest lighted candles with a match. And there, too, were twenty Americans, retirees, former college students, friends from the bars and cantinas.

Atticus knelt to pray and slid his hat underneath the chair. After he was sitting, Renata softly came up from behind him and laid a hand on his shoulder. She wore an informal black silk jacket and full print skirt, and a perfume he thought might have been the kind Serena wore. She kissed his cheek and said, "I'm not Catholic. Is it okay if I sit up here?"

"Oh sure." She sat and he felt her forearm gently touch his own and not flinch away. And he found himself fondly gazing at a face that was haloed by the brilliant stained-glass windows. "You clean up real good," he whispered.

She flushed and smiled.

A girl of no more than eight sashayed up and down the nave with a wide push broom that skidded on top of a towel. The high altar held a six-foot-high statue of Christ in his funeral sheet, floating out of his sepulchre and looking up to

Heaven. Awkwardly pictured on the great wall behind him were choirs of angels, white clouds, and blue sky. And in the high altar's sacristy was a glaring Mayan boy of seventeen or so in a grayed white western shirt and frayed blue jeans. Atticus wasn't sure if it was himself the kid was staring at or not, and then finally the heat in his look flamed out and he withdrew.

Renata was prim beside him. Without emotion. She stared at the painted black coffin as though she were a photograph of stillness and moderation. And then a priest in black vestments walked to the Saint Joseph side altar and all the people stood up. The priest crossed himself and raised up his hands in order to invoke God's presence, saying the word *Señor* for "Lord," but only a few people there knew the Spanish responses.

Colorado was in his head, Saint Mary's church bright and beautiful and filled to bursting with his neighbors and friends, Serena in the pink casket and Frank holding up pretty good while Scott fell apart with tears, his hands held to his face through the funeral, fourteen black stitches above his left eyebrow, a hard plastic neck brace on. Their hands happened to touch at the funeral and Atticus never forgave himself for sliding his hand away.

Stuart went up to the front at the gospel and interpreted in English as the priest read from Saint John: how Jesus wept when he heard Lazarus was dead, and then ordered the stone to be taken away from the tomb, and cried out for Lazarus to come forth. And Lazarus came forth, bound hand and foot with graveclothes, so that Jesus said to loosen the windings and let Lazarus go free.

And then, for the homily, Stuart Chandler hooked on heavy black spectacles and unfolded a sheet of paper that trembled in his hands. Without looking up, he said, "I'll be reading a hymn from the Madrid Codex, a hymn that was sung in the City of the Gods, Teotihuacán, in the presence of the dead." And he read: " 'Thus the dead were addressed when they died. If it was a man, they spoke to him, invoked him as a divine being, in the name of a pheasant; if it was a woman, in the name of owl; and they said to them: 'Awaken, already the sky is tinged with red, already the dawn has come, already the flame-colored pheasants are singing, the fire-colored swallows, already the butterflies are on the wing.' For this reason the ancient ones said, he who has died, he becomes a god. They said: 'He became a god there,' which means that he died.' "

And then there was the cemetery. The cemetery. And skull candles on some graves, teacups of candies, a carnival of piping and crepe and shot-glass votive lights, crucifixes at angles in the blond grass, rosaries like string neckties on the gray stones, a full toy shop of Jesus and Mary dolls. Twenty people stood around an open pit in the one P.M. sun, talking about practical matters, saying hello to old friends; and Atticus kept telling himself it was only temporary, the box would be raised up, the body shipped, and his son would be put to rest on Coyote Hill where the Dutch elm looked like a cleaning woman hanging up sheets in the wind. The Mexican priest said in unfamiliar Spanish the Catholic prayers of burial that were too familiar to Atticus, and then the priest stepped away and the crowd broke apart and kind people Atticus didn't know said good-bye or wished they could've met him under happier circumstances.

Renata waited until he raised up from a last prayer and then said, "We have the day."

"What I'd like to do is look at his studio."

She hesitated before saying, "Yes. Good idea."

She took him in the old red Volkswagen, halt-ingly riding through Resurrección. Renata got out of her silk jacket and shifted to second gear in order to go around a box-framed garbage truck that up north would have been used to ship hogs. A heavy man in green hip waders was standing knee-deep in a high tonnage of trash, sorting whiskey bottles, looking into a car battery and stacking it next to a crippled electric fan, ripping off the back of a radio in order to poke the tubes inside.

She stopped at the intersection of Avenida de la Independencia and the gray highway. A policeman in dark blue and sunglasses was sitting on a motorcycle just off the pavement, giving her a hard stare. Renata grew nervous and the Volkswagen stalled while still at the stop sign. She said, "This car doesn't idle, it loiters."

"Looks like he was trying to spiff it up at least."

"Oh?" She waggled the gear shift into neutral and turned the ignition as she stared across the highway at the policeman.

His knuckles knocked twice against the front windshield. "You got some new glass here. You can tell from the rubber seal."

She turned south onto the highway and looked into the rearview mirror. "Scott bought the car from a kid who got caught smuggling *ganja* in from Belize."

"And what would *ganja* be in English?"

"Marijuana."

"Oh." His thumbnail gently lifted up a see-through sticker for Pittsburgh Plate Glass that was high up in the right-hand corner. "You can have the car if you want it."

"Seriously?"

"Don't expect it would make it far as the border, and selling it — Well, I'd be happy to know you'd put it to good use."

She shifted to fourth gear as she said, "That's really very nice of you. Thank you."

"You're welcome."

They rode in silence for a few minutes and then he asked, "The kid who sold him the car, is he here still?"

She frowned at him. "Hangs out on the beach, I think. Why?"

"Wondering; that's all."

She smiled. "You do have a busy mind."

"Well, I try not to." Atticus looked out his open side window at some pretty, preteen girls squatting in the dry weeds of a bus stop, licking the hot pepper sauce on pork rinds. Horseflies were walking around their mouths and their skirts were lifted up over their knees for the breeze. And then there was nothing but jungle and the scraggle of gray rock and charred black stumps and the fragile cornstalks that meant agriculture in that poor soil. Atticus kept thinking about the things Renata ought to have been telling him, the grief and unhappiness she ought to have expressed. She seemed flippant and preoccupied, and that was it. *Oh, did he die? What a shame.* No pain or misery or regret, nothing of what Atticus was feeling. Having gone along the highway for ten minutes, Renata slowed the Volkswagen until she saw a red flag hanging from one of a thousand just-alike trees. She then turned east onto a green alley that was being overgrown by hothouse plants that sought the rods of sunlight angling down through the green ceiling of leaves overhead. Exotic birds darted a few yards away and alighted. A great-beaked toucan jittered its legs on a high branch but didn't open its wings. Iguanas were in the orange ruts of the road, getting information about the engine noise and then scattering wildly into the weeds or lumbering just off the road and following them with a tiny eye that was like a purple bead on a necklace. High grasses slashed away under the bumper, and dry sticks screeched along the doors so that Atticus had to raise his voice to ask, "How'd he find this place?"

Renata yelled back, "Eduardo, the shaman. I guess he's a neighbor."

And then they were in sunlight and green savannah and a sky as blue as shoe prints in the snow. Renata braked the car and killed the engine, and Atticus could hear the surge and groan and spray of a Caribbean sea just out of sight. "And now we walk," she said. She pressed her high-heeled shoes off against the floorboard and then got out to unfasten her full skirt as Atticus took off his hot black cashmere coat and gray silk tie. She dug around in the back for other clothing and got into some cardinal red Stanford gym shorts and an overlarge white oxford shirt. A garden spade was there for some reason. She smiled at him and said, "I didn't know Americans still wore braces."

"They're galluses," he said.

"It's a very smart fashion statement."

"Antelope's in the *vanguard* of high fashion. A lot of people don't know that."

She walked ahead of him but paused when she saw Atticus was staring at the right front fender.

"Was there an accident?" he asked.

She didn't say.

"Wasn't that perfect a match on the color is how I knew." Hunching by the car, he swam his right hand over the surface, then got a penknife from his pocket and skidded the blade on a fender edge so a half-inch of red paint peeled up like the skin of an apple. "You got a paint job here that's maybe a week, two weeks old. See how it peels up? Hasn't set yet or it'd flake off."

"Okay; you convinced me."

Atticus shot her a rankled look.

"You knew he was a lousy driver," Renata said.

Atticus hunched there with his hands on his knees as if he'd lost his wind. And then he straightened. "Yes, I did."

"We don't have to go up there."

"We do," he said, and they lunged through grass that was as high as their knees to the foot of a steep hill that was topped by a *casita* made of upright bamboo poles and palm thatching.

102

Electrical power lines looped out from the roof and over the upper parts of some trees. On the way up, Renata moved some grass aside with her right foot in order to show Atticus a square gray stone with a fierce eagle carved in it. Only then did he notice the crannies and juts and lintels and stair steps that appeared to be growing out of the emerald green of the hill.

"Are they ruins?"

"A Mayan lookout post. Have you been to Chichén Itzá?"

"Yep."

"Four or five thousand foreigners clawing their way up the Temple of Kukulkán, echoing 'Hello' in the ball court, having pictures taken of their heads between the jaws of the plumed serpent. So much for archaeological preservation. Here the Mayans wised up and kept the place secret."

Atticus paused on the way up and held his hands on his hips. He was panting and his open white shirt was grayly spotted with sweat. Renata turned. "Higher than it looks," he told her.

She went up a few steps more and he followed her, getting the tang of seaweed and salt air as he attained the top. His heart was hammering high in his chest with the fresh, winter pain that he hadn't yet gotten used to.

Renata asked, "Are you okay?"

"Hell, I'm sixty-seven years old. Haven't been

103

okay since I was fifty."

"Your heart?"

"Carburetor trouble," he said. "Whole thing gets to acting like a juvenile delinquent at times, kicking hard at the door. Don't ever have to say 'Who's there?' " He smiled for the sake of Renata's frightened brown eyes and squinted farther on at the sea view. From that height he could see the white coastline in its twists and tangles around *bahías* and *bajas* along the way north to Cancún. East was the navy blue of the Gulf Stream and the sea changing to azure and finally a lime-juice green as it overran a higher shelf of the coast and blasted into coffee-colored rocks. They were on a gray cathedral of stone, and west was green jungle and low plains and swamp that hazily blued at twenty miles and made the jungle seem no more than cigarette smoke rising up into the horizon. "Pretty out here," he said.

"Yes, it is."

He turned to see Renata holding the handle of the door, and then translated the Spanish on a sign that the Mexican police had stapled onto the wood, promising jail to looters and trespassers. *Crime scene,* he thought. "Didn't have a lock on the door?" he asked.

She stared at a hasp where a padlock ought to have been. "Oh, I forgot. Wednesday Scott told me there was a break-in here. Kids, probably.

Stuart's house has been hit three times."

"We got an old house on the ranch," he said. "Even hunters use it. Hard to keep people off your property if you aren't always there to protect it." She smiled at him for some reason; he presumed he was wearing what Scott used to call his Republican face.

Renata pulled the door and then interpreted Atticus's hesitation. "Don't worry. We've cleaned it up a little."

They walked inside. East was a wall of upright bamboo that was hinged in order to create huge doors that could open the interior to the light and air of the seascape or could be wired shut to the roof supports for weather protection. Renata unscrewed the wires and pushed the hinged bamboo out, making the twelve-by-twenty house as open as an unscreened porch. Atticus held up the Radiola tape player he'd given Scott at Christmas. A homemade copy of Linda Ronstadt's *Canciones de mi Padre* was at the end of its reel. "You'd think they'd've stolen this."

"Who?"

"You said kids broke in here."

She gave it some thought and finally said, "Useless to them, probably. Most campesinos don't have electricity in their homes."

"Oh. Uh huh." Atticus put the tape player down. "You forget where you are." His eyes found a green wingback chair like his at home that was angled toward the door.

Renata went over to it and grazed her hand along the leather back. "He was sitting here," she said. "Slumped over to the right. His fingers nearly touched the floor. And the gun was only an inch away."

"Were there pictures taken?"

"I have no idea."

Atticus frowned. "You weren't here with the police?"

"I hate blood," she said. "Seeing it makes me ill."

"So: What? You peeked in, thought 'Oh my gosh, blood,' and skipped off?"

She seemed stunned by his irritation. She seemed to retreat a little, and there was a shine of tears in her eyes as she said, "I figured this would be hard for you." She paused, as if phrasing a further explanation, but simply told him, "I have to get out of here." And then she was out of the house and heading down to the sea.

Atticus strolled toward a stone fireplace and a white enamel pantry table that was topped by a gas camp stove. A full pot of coffee was still on it and smelled of having scorched on the heat. Whiskey glasses were upside down on a dish-towel. The gray iron sink had cold and hot water taps and held a jar of turpentine full of paint-brushes that smoked with green and indigo colors when he touched them. Overhead were track lights that could swing any which way, with four angled down on a big paint-stained easel with nothing on it and the green wingback chair that he couldn't look at. A humming refrigerator was cooling *agua mineral* and Coca-Colas, a paper bag of Columbian coffee grounds, a package of Mexican sugar pastries, and a string bag of oranges. A half-full ice cube tray was in the freezer. The kitchen counter held an empty Coca-Cola can that Atticus was about to pitch in the trash when he felt its not-hotness and figured that it had been finished less than an hour ago. He looked at the floor. Wet shoe prints were faintly there that the high humidity had failed to dry, and a few places elsewhere there was sand. Kids? Squatters? The merely curious? He crushed the Coca-Cola can in his right hand and tossed it.

Walking across the room he found a palette knife that had fallen to the floor and a hairline furrow of blood between the floorboards a good four feet away from the chair. He got to his feet and tried to forget the ugly picture he'd imagined, looking out at the long sabers of sunglancing greenery clattering in the breeze. His hands touched a jumble of oil paints that were pitched all over the butcher paper on the worktable like squeezed-up toothpaste containers. And there was a big wooden palette with oil paints that he let his fingers touch. All the titanium white and cerulian blue had been scraped away with a putty knife, but the alizarine crimson, Prussian blue, and dark green were still moist, their skins yielding like thin plastic. It surprised him that he knew the proper names for the colors; he hadn't known he'd picked them up over those many years.

Wide closets of white, louvered doors made up much of one wall, and inside them were simple carpenter's tools and a mitre box and a stack of one-bys a guy could make wooden picture frames with. Canvas was rolled up in the second closet in tubes of four sizes, and some prestretched panels were sitting against big cans of gesso that were grayly veiled by spiderwebs. The fancy walnut case that the shotgun came in was on the floor, and a gun-cleaning kit was in an unopened cardboard box. Hidden behind the third closet was a white porcelain toilet and a lavatory with soap in a plastic tray but without any towels on the wooden bars. A black Speedo swimsuit drooped over a hook. In the medicine cabinet were bicarbonate of soda, headache pills, cough syrup, aspirin, peroxide, insect repellent, and lithium. A Jameson's whiskey carton was in the trash can. Atticus smelled blood and then he saw in a tin pail some white underpants made pink with the work of wiping the floor.

Atticus went out of the bathroom and out of the house, walking to the green verge high above the cove, looking down at wild oleander and a household something, a shoe, flung into a bush, and farther on a sheer drop to churning water that was as clear as a canning jar. Renata was there, hunting shells he guessed, and he found himself staring at her nakedness as she sloshed out of the sea and twisted her hair and gingerly collected her clothes. He tried hard to feature himself having the gall to swim in those circumstances, but he seemed to lack the imagination.

Atticus got the Radiola tape player, fastened the door, and then skidded down the hill, holding his free hand out to keep from falling. Renata was sitting against the Volkswagen bumper, rolling her white oxford sleeves up over her elbows, blithe as a teenager with people who didn't matter. "Enjoy your *dip?*" he asked.

"Quite," she said. She felt his heat and faced him with the fierce concentration of a good student who'd been fretting her sentences for a while. "You have to remember that he was my friend," she said. "And he let me find him like that. I feel used. Violated. I'm finding it hard to imagine his suicide as anything but a horrible act of aggression."

Atticus thought better of his anger and just walked around to the right of the car and got in. Everything was beginning to seem wrong to him. Emotionally off. Renata got in and turned the key in the ignition, and there was a sheen to her eyes that was such good acting he wanted to congratulate her for it. He looked out the side window.

"Don't see his motorcycle," he said.

"The police have it. *Evidencia*. Stuart can get his things from the authorities and ship them to Colorado. You'll probably want us to sell his Harley though, won't you?"

"Oh, I expect."

She asked, "Are you thinking of flying out tomorrow?"

She seemed pleased when he said yes.

She backed the car up and cranked it around onto the overgrown road. And then she just drove until they got to the highway. She looked to the right and left, letting a pink hotel jeep go past, as she asked, "Have you heard how Scott and I found each other the first time?"

"Scott probably told me that once. I forgot."

She floored the car and got onto the highway ahead of a truck that held its position no more than four feet behind her for a half mile or more. The truck finally fell back and Renata focused again on the highway. She said, "A girlfriend of mine killed herself in the house attic when I was twenty and in Paris, and I felt like suicide was a door she'd left open for me. I began hearing these voices inside my head. 'You're a slut, you know.' 'You're so stupid.' All in high-pitched, frightening French. I figured the voices wouldn't follow me if I was in an English-speaking country, so I signed on for classes again at Sarah Lawrence. But the voices were in English now, and giving me orders that I felt I had to obey. 'Scream.' 'Hide in the closet.' 'Don't talk.' 'Hit that window with your fist.' A housemate found out I was wearing long-sleeved shirts because I was purposely scalding my left wrist and arm with hot coffee every morning. The first psychiatrist I saw asked me if I masturbated with my left hand. I howled and howled at that; I thought it was the funniest thing I'd ever heard. I was finally hauled into Hirsch Clinic when police found me sitting with the pigeons in Washington Square in New York, completely unable to speak or to move, but hearing voices that said 'Sit here and be still.' "

She hurriedly shifted from fourth to third and Atticus faced front as Renata's foot hit the brake gently at first and then harder. An old green Chevrolet pickup truck whose hood and fenders flapped like shingles was turtling ahead with its huge haul of ten or more hotel workers going in for the four o'clock shift. "I hate this highway," she said. "Kids are getting killed on it all the time. And the fatalists here simply put up more crosses."

She peered into her rearview mirror and Atticus craned his head around. "Okay, go," he told her. She floored it and passed the truck before she shifted to fourth. She seemed lost in thought so he urged her with, "Hearing voices that said, 'Sit here and be still.' And then being hauled into Hirsch."

111

"Oh, thanks. I felt I was trapped inside a foreign body that frustrated all my attempts to operate it. I used to hear the psychiatrist asking me questions, but a half hour or more would pass before I would finally answer him and then he'd have gone off to another patient. Hospital interns used to peer at me with fascination as he lifted my arm up from my side and let me hold it there, still as a post, as he lectured. And then when he finished explaining my condition, he'd pull down my arm again. My eyes were as dull and blank and fake as a shark's, and I was stiff and silent and seemingly not with it, but I heard and saw and perceived in ways I haven't since I became normal.

"And that's how I was when I first met Scott. I forget the circumstances of why I was outside my room or why he was in the hall, but he was and I was, at three or four in the morning. I was just sitting in a fold-down chair by an iron-barred window. Catatonic. And Scott was talking to me like no one had in a while, as if we were on our first date. Hour after hour of fetchingly manic talk, no letting up; he'd finished the complete works of Shakespeare at Hirsch and thought old Will was pretty good. His favorite cereal as a kid was Cheerios, but now he liked wheat germ and yogurt; his favorite movie was *King Kong*, or maybe *Singin' in the Rain*; his favorite novel was *Beau Geste*, he was sure of that, but nobody but

Scott had read it, he said, they just thought they had. He told me his favorite person in the twentieth century was Albert Schweitzer — whom he said you resembled — and if he were about to be executed he'd order a Waldorf salad, medium rare prime rib, mashed potatoes, and apple cobbler."

"His mother would fix him that for his birthdays."

"Really?" She flicked the Volkswagen's blinker and waited for a high-balling tanker to blow past before she turned left. "Even today," she said, "as insane as I was, I remember practically every word. He told me he was a chronic manic depressive, but full of enough false beliefs and obsessions to fit the paranoid schizophrenic type, and for a time found himself hooked on Thorazine, so he knew what it was like to be inside a straitjacket." She smiled and turned to Atticus. "And he was such a *boy* about competition. Scott told me he was the best patient there but the psychiatrists wouldn't say so for fear of playing favorites."

Atticus ticked his head. "Yep, that's him all right."

She said, "He further informed me that I'd be freed from the locked ward when I could fill out my food menu for the day, and I could get off the fifth floor when I finished my first pair of moccasins. And then it was sunrise and it was just glorious. We both stared at it for a minute, and he tried to entertain me by singing 'Here Comes the Sun.' Have you heard it, by the Beatles?"

"I haven't been feeble *all* my life."

She sang: " 'Little darling, it's been a long, cold, lonely winter. Little darling, it seems like years since it's been clear. Here comes the sun. Doont-n-doo-doo. Here comes the sun. And it's all right.' "

She shifted to third and fought the bumps as she turned onto an unpaved road through the *barrio*. She said, "I have no idea how I looked, but Scott later said my face was different, unfrozen, and he unfolded a chair beside mine and held me in his arms as if we were sweethearts and he sang the whole song again. And it was amazing. I found myself seeing colors for the first time. Yellow, pink, green, and blue. Up until then there'd only been monochrome, gray and white. And I kept hearing him singing over and over again, 'And it's all right.' I fell in love with Scott Cody then and there. And I felt all my life I'd owe him. And I'd be honored to do whatever he asked."

Renata was expected at the bookstore to help out, so she dropped Atticus off at Scott's place and promised to return that night. Atticus forgot the Radiola tape player atop the refrigerator as he opened a half-frozen Coca-Cola that he took upstairs to the high-tech desk. And he found underneath it in a plastic wastebasket a Mexican newspaper, *El Anunciador*, from the first of the week. Atticus got out of his hot funeral clothes and rummaged through four drawers of the high armoire until he found some black running shorts to put on as trunks, and he felt the toll of a hard day as he trudged downstairs and outside to the pool, holding the folded *diario* and a Spanish dictionary under his arm. The half-smoked cigarette he'd seen that morning on the upstairs railing had fallen to the hot tiles. The lettering on it read "Salem." Stuart's brand. He'd been up in the bedroom, then. Atticus worried about that as he sat in a white deck chair and shaded his eyes to look at a four o'clock sun that wasn't letting up. Sports was the easiest newspaper Spanish to translate, so he stayed on that page for a while, reading about winter baseball, and then he looked at a furniture ad, at the interest rates offered by Bancomex, and at page 8 where a paragraph had been carefully cut out of the obituaries. Who? he wondered. And then he closed his eyes. He felt faint and poorly all of a sudden. His stomach hurt and his head floated and when he pressed it his skin showed a yellow imprint that soon was pink with sunburn again. He got up and walked over to the deep end of the pool and pinched his nose and jumped into the water, as upright as a plank. He swam across the pool and back in the sloppy way of a boy just learning how. And then he just hung on to the pool ladder, feeling woozy, and got out, and he'd walked into the kitchen for a seltzer when he heard a faint knocking at the front door.

Yesterday afternoon's taxi driver was there on the other side of it, smiling as if Atticus were good fortune itself. What was his name? Panchito? His hand was soft as a fish as he shook the cattleman's hand and talked importantly in Spanish.

Even the phrase to say he knew little Spanish was locked up. "Afraid I don't know what you're talking about."

Panchito thought for a bit and got a Lufthansa flight packet from inside his shirt and held it up so Atticus would see Scott's name printed on it. *"Cotzi,"* he said. And then he pointed at Atticus. "Señor Cody?"

"Sí." He recalled that "his" in Spanish was *su.* *"Su padre."*

Panchito offered the flight packet to him, and Atticus found inside a one-way first-class ticket for a flight from Mexico City to Frankfurt, Germany. The flight was to have been Thursday night at nine-twenty and was charged on Wednesday to Scott's American Express card in feminine handwriting. *Germany!* he thought. "Was this phoned in?" he asked.

"No se," the Mexican said, but whether he did

not know the answer or he did not know the English wasn't clear. Panchito talked for a full minute then, but Atticus was too tired to make sense of it; he simply looked and looked at the flight packet and felt too slow to figure it out. Everything was wrong. When Panchito finished his paragraph and faced him expectantly, Atticus finally said, *"Muy gracias."* Very thanks. And then he got out his wallet and handed Panchito a five-dollar bill.

Panchito was formal in folding the bill inside his own wallet. Atticus frowned at him and said, "My son was going to Germany, but then he changed his mind and killed himself."

Panchito hesitantly smiled.

"Happens all the time," Atticus said. "Some people hate to fly."

And then he shut the front door on the taxi driver, furious now with everyone and knowing he was going to be sick. Getting upstairs was as much an agony as if he'd worked a twenty-hour day, and the hallway seemed to yaw as he swayed along it and into Scott's room. Atticus sagged to his knees by the black toilet bowl and just about fainted with nausea. And then the poisons surged up from him and he seemed to smell the horrible stink within the painted coffin. The floor was winter to his skin as he knelt there for five minutes more and flew his sickness into the toilet again, and then he tilted to the high wide bed and fell face forward on it just as he would have as a kid. Within the next few hours he went to the bathroom a half-dozen times, and then he passed out and heard Renata say from a great distance, "Are you okay?" She fitted right into the past and Serena looking out the upstairs window, saying how pretty the evening was. His wife heaved up the sash for the fresh spring breeze, and Atticus helped Serena flip over Scotty's crib mattress in order to hide the stains. And in his dream those stains were blood and he was in the dining room and gunsmoke floated against the ceiling and hundreds of wineglasses filled the table and red wine was spilling onto the rug and it hurt his stomach to see it. "You oughta be careful," Atticus said. And a friend of his son's told Atticus, "We all live on the fringe here. We make up the rules as we go along." And handwriting was on the dining room mirror, handwriting in lipstick, and then he heard Renata say from outside his head, "If you wanted to stay for a few more days, you could've just told us. You didn't have to get *el turista* on our account."

Atticus opened his eyes and it was night and Renata Isaacs was sitting on the bed, her palm as cool as a washcloth to his brow. And he felt the influence of his flesh as he found himself summoning up how it was to hold her as she wept.

"Don't," he said. "I'll be all right."

"Actually I like paying attention to people

when they're sick. Helps to compensate for my thoroughgoing malice toward them when they're healthy."

"How late is it?"

"Nine."

He sighed and said, "Sorry, but I've gotta get up again," and Renata helped him ease himself up from a damp sheet. His legs jellied a little, but he could walk into the bathroom by tilting into the gray wall. She turned away from his nakedness, and then he heard her sliding the floor-to-ceiling glass doors to let in the good night air. As he ran the tap water to brush his teeth, he could hear her saying, "I know how impossible it is for you now, but if you could step back from your misery you'd find your sickness rather interesting really. I mean by that, the extremes your body goes to to get rid of the poisons."

" 'Extremes' is pretty mild," he said. "It's more like 'counterrevolutionary.' " Atticus got Pepto-Bismol from the medicine cabinet and swallowed an inch of it straight from the bottle, then showered and some minutes later walked out, buttoning up his pajamas.

She was standing by the bookcase with a collection of Mexican poetry. She watched him haltingly get onto the bed. She said, "You're white as a ghost."

"Won't last forever, I expect."

"You should sleep," Renata said, and fluffed

his pillow and tucked the blanket over his horse-man's legs.

Atticus tried to put some affection in his smile, but he was impatient with himself for his need for feminine tenderness, because his ache and poisoning and how he felt now was not half as important as his fierce certainty that his son had been murdered.

FOUR

Sandhills. Snow. Gray weather. And Scott up from Mexico for the holidays, in a tan hunting coat but no hunting gun, sleepily riding Pepper with his hands holding his Radiola tape player against the saddle. The horses lazily plodded along a coulee in the oil patch, and Patsy Cline was singing "Crazy." And then the sun and its twin were high overhead like Communion hosts and Atticus said, "You call that a sundog." His son peered up and asked, "How can you tell which is sun and which is dog?" And then Scott turned his head so his father could see that his face was shot off.

Atticus jerked awake and figured out where he was. Warm air fattened the drapes, and their pull cords tapped against the gray wall. His *Spanish for Travellers* was in his hand and his mouth was as dry as a shoe. Atticus could hear the clanking of pots and pans in the kitchen and then the gong and sigh of tap water filling a kettle. He made another woozy trip to the bathroom and found a red lipsticked message on the bathroom mirror: "Police at 1." He showered and got into his robe.

Renata was in the kitchen speaking a Spanish he couldn't make out, and then she was coming upstairs. And he was sitting up on the bed when she rapped lightly on the door and then pushed it, appearing with a bottle of Coca-Cola and a squat glass that was jagged with ice. She wore high-fashion blue jeans beneath an untucked and overlarge white oxford shirt. The fumes of tobacco smoke seemed to float from her clothes. She said, "You probably think you're dying, but you're not."

"As sicknesses go, this one packs a wallop. I've been pretty basic with myself the past few hours."

She seriously poured the cola into the glass and gave it to him with one white pill. "Lomotil. From Stuart's pharmacopoeia. I'll have to get you some more." She paused. "I couldn't find any Diet Coke."

Atticus smiled. "I'll try not to worry about the calories." He took the pill and finished half of the Coke.

"Shall I call the airline and cancel your flight?"

"Yeah. I'm too raggedy for travel right now."

Renata sat at his feet and folded her arms underneath her breasts just as Serena would when she focused on the family pictures and talked about the full day ahead. She said, "You know, the Mexicans get it, too. Children who seem to

122

be five and six years old are often actually eight and nine. Especially in the jungle there's a big problem with intestinal parasites and tuberculosis. Americans go home and get over it. Here you get used to it or die."

A kitchen drawer was pulled out and pushed shut. "Who's that?" he asked.

"Stuart, or María. I met her in the *jardín.* She's making a healing potion."

"A potion. You think it'll work?"

Renata shrugged and said, "When I was eight and living in Europe, I got some warts on my fingers. A family doctor told me to put my hands on a green machine in his office, and he turned on the motor and my skin tingled for a few seconds. And then he winked and said the green machine had cured me. And my warts were gone in a week."

Lufthansa, he found himself thinking. A flight to Germany. "You're only eight for so long," Atticus said.

"Unfortunately." Renata got up and created a purpose for getting up by walking across the room and causing the draperies to sweep aside. The sky was just as blue as yesterday or the day before that, and the sunglare on the snow-white stucco was as bright as the oncoming lights of a car. She said, "The hotel boys are playing soccer." And she said, "White sand gets on their skin and they look like sugared doughnuts."

"¡Está listo!" María called.

Renata turned. "She says it's ready. Shall she bring it up?"

"Kind of funky up here. You go on ahead." She walked out as Atticus went into the gray bathroom again. And Stuart was at the dining room table, fanning pink and yellow wildflowers out on an unfolded newspaper, when Atticus painstakingly stepped downstairs in his suit pants and a fresh white shirt, one big hand patting along the stairway banister in case his legs mellowed or his feet slipped. Stuart looked up and feigned disappointment. "Bad luck about the illness."

"Where's Renata?"

"The pharmacy," he said. "Well. You seem to be ambulatory."

"Just let me get my skates." Stuart was barefoot on the pink marble, and Atticus remembered that there had been an Indian rug in the photograph of the dining room. Was it stolen? He asked, "You know what happened to the rug that was here?"

Stuart frowned at the dining room floor. "I haven't the foggiest."

María walked out of the kitchen with a four- or five-month-old baby boy and a kettle. *"Buenas tardes, señor."*

"Buenas."

"¿Cómo está usted?"

Atticus lost the little Spanish he had, but María

just saddled the baby on her left hip as she tipped the kettle into a whiskey glass.

Stuart said, "She brought you a tea from her *abuelo*. Her shaman. She says it's made from the bark of a tree."

"Takinche," María said.

"A *takinche* tree. And possibly eye of newt."

Atticus held a whiskey glass that seemed to contain hot root beer and a skin of woodbits that looked like nothing more than shredded tea leaves. Without a second thought he drank the concoction, trying not to taste it, but tasting and tasting it.

"Aren't you manly," Stuart said.

Atticus wiped the gray wings of his mustache with his palm as he grinned at María and told her, "I feel better already."

María flushed with shyness and hooded her son with her shawl. Stuart spoke in Spanish, seeming to ask María about the rug, but María simply shrugged and replied, *"No sé, señor."* Don't know.

"Well, that's better than my maid," Stuart said. "She'd tell you it never existed."

María headed for the front door and she smiled and said, *"Hasta mañana."* She giggled at Stuart's Spanish reply and Atticus found himself registering how long Stuart fondly gazed at her as she went out.

Atticus's hand held on to the headpiece of a

dining room chair as the floor seemed to tip. "Are the police coming here or I am going there?"

"Renata's taking you." He paused. *"La comisaría de policía."*

"Thanks. I was about to ask."

"I hope you're not expecting answers," Stuart said, "because the police here don't always dot all the *i*'s and cross all the *t*'s, if you get my meaning. Mexican fatalism gets jumbled up with a lot of the police being illiterate, and a few of them are dreadful people besides, not to put too fine a point on it. Half the time the police can't get the facts right, and half the time they just don't care to." Stuart got some garden scissors from the sideboard as he said, "Anyway, your son's clothing and shotgun are there. And the motorcycle. Will you be able to ride it back?"

"Oh, I reckon."

Stuart snipped some wildflowers and plunked them into a jar. "We could hire someone to roll it here."

"I feel that *takinche* kicking in already."

"Renata and I were hoping to have you over for dinner tonight. You probably think that sounds perfectly awful now, but I'm fairly sure you'll be hungry by six. We'll have something mild, fettucine or a risotto."

"Real neighborly," he said.

He smiled. "You can say that without irony! Aren't you *quaint!*"

"You know medicines?"

Stuart looked at him oddly.

He heavily sat down on the dining room chair. "Why I said that is Renata used a word: pharmacopoeia? Means you know about pills and such, I take it."

Stuart blinked slowly and said, "What a pity that I do."

Atticus shifted to the right and got out his wallet from his trousers pocket. Tucked under a flap was the pharmacy receipt María found on the bathroom floor upstairs. He held it out to Stuart. "You know what this would be for?"

He read it quickly and a shade seemed to go down in his face. He hobbied as he said, "We have cancer cures here, quote unquote, that you can't get in the United States. And if you're desperate enough, you get a prescription for that. Whose is it?"

"Was it Scott's?"

"We'd have known if Scott was that ill, wouldn't we?"

Atticus smoothed his hair with his hand. "Well, I've seen people who keep it pretty quiet. Don't want to make a fuss. You know."

"That hardly describes your son, does it." Stuart shifted flowers in the jar until he seemed satisfied, and then he gathered the cuttings into his hand as he said, "We were desperate rivals, Scott and I. We fought all the time."

"You were both in love with the same woman."

"Can't fool you." He went into the kitchen and threw the flower cuttings into the trash. He said from the kitchen, "She has *complete* power over me. I find it frustrating, but I presume it was just as frustrating for Scott." Stuart folded his arms at the doorway. "One thing I'll always regret is the twinge of *gladness* I felt when I heard he was dead." High color flushed his face. "Common decency deserts me on occasion." He tried to smile, but his mouth trembled. "Even now, for example."

Atticus fiercely stared at him and then offered, "You do try to be honest, don't you."

"Rude is more like it, I'm afraid." Stuart put his hands on a dining room chair and faced him squarely as he said, "*I* have cancer." He put on a happy face as he held up his pack of Salem cigarettes like it was show-and-tell, then frowned as he shook one out and flipped the pack back onto the dining room table.

"I'm real sorry."

"Well *I'm* angry. Absolutely furious, if truth be told. I guess I'm in the first stage of grief."

"Have you told Renata?"

"Oh, that would be fetching, wouldn't it." He dug out a fancy lighter from his front pants pocket, got a flame, hungrily inhaled on the cigarette, and coughed wrackingly. His face was crimson as he said, *"Quod erat demonstrandum."*

Atticus was silent, and then he asked, "Where were you Wednesday night?"

Stuart faced him with wonder and then forced a laugh. "My God, you're *detecting! You're a sleuth!"*

Atticus just stared.

Stuart inhaled his cigarette again and funneled smoke out the side of his mouth. "With Renata and Scott at The Scorpion and at the Marriott for the fiesta and the Williams play. And then I went to the bookstore and finished up some paperwork."

"You there for a long time?"

"Yes, from about ten o'clock to one-thirty or so. Tweaking the debits and credits, if you must know. My financial shape isn't any more healthy than I am. My thanks in advance for your sympathy." Stuart got an ashtray from the kitchen and gently carved the ash from his cigarette. "Are you trying to establish if I have an alibi?"

"Yep."

"I have none. Shall I expect you to *grill* me further?"

The front door opened and Renata called, *"¡Hola!"*

Stuart whispered, "And now, for the sake of the children, we pretend nothing's happened."

Renata walked in, looking harried, her mind

elsewhere, with a white sack from the *farmacia* in her hand. "More Lomotil," she said. "How are you now?"

"Sitting up and taking notice," he said, and got up from the dining room chair. "I'll go fetch my hat."

Stuart may have spoken about their talk while he was upstairs, because Renata drove Atticus through the *centro* in silence — so daughterly that silence, as if she'd been wrongly punished and thought a sentence might heal the rift she wanted prolonged. She finally said, "I hate it when he talks about me."

"Wasn't much said."

"Stuart has this unfunny way of teasing, playing the British twit, the scoundrel, the thoroughgoing cad. I find it defensive and maddening." Renata shifted down to first gear as a Bohemia beer truck lumbered into her lane, then impatiently shifted to second to swerve around it and was halted again by the white cart of a man hawking chicharrones. "You haven't seen his good side. Stuart's really a Renaissance man. He's good at business, he's suave, he's fluent in five languages, he's practically a walking library. And he's *sane*. Stability was a big plus for me."

"You're trying to tell me why you chose him over Scott. You can't put that sort of thing into words."

She glanced at his face and again fronted her glare. "I find the choice so foolish sometimes. Even hellish. But he has such *power* over me. I hate it."

"He said the same thing about you."

"Really? I haven't felt in charge at all."

"Well, I believe that. Seems to me every one of you here oughta try living according to Bible values and see how *that* works out."

Renata sighed.

"Well, I had to say it."

She parked the Volkswagen near the shaded porches of the shops on the west side of the *jardín*. A public telephone was bolted to a great pillar there, and a shoeshine boy stood on his box as he pretended to make a call. His friends grinned as he shouted, *"Quisiera denunciar un carterista. Un cochino enano."* Atticus couldn't translate it. *Un carterista,* he thought, was a pickpocket.

Renata said, "I found the car here. Where we're parked." She got out.

Teenaged boys were busily soaping and rinsing cars in the street while the American owners skeptically watched. On the great plaza of the *parroquia,* twenty grandfatherly men in white shirts and trousers were tuning the instruments of an orchestra, and Stuart's beggar was behind them there, swinging forward on his crutches and his one leg until he got to the back of the *parro-*

quia and abruptly disappeared as if through a held-open door.

Atticus followed Renata under the loggia in front of Printers Inc, which was closed, and toward a grand but foundering city hall and *la comisaría de policía.* Half a dozen frowning teenagers in hand-me-down navy blue uniforms defended the police station with machine guns and fifty-year-old rifles that they seemed eager to try out.

Renata was waiting at the street corner for the halting passage of a hotel tour bus filled with Americans his age in golf visors and sunglasses. A fairly young mother knelt on the sidewalk with a feeding infant at her left breast, and she talked to Renata with a face full of such frank misery that Renata put a peso bill in the upraised hand and got a pack of Chiclets from an offered box. "I have zero discipline. Zilch," Renata said. "You always feel so guilty. Stuart has the right idea."

"I just saw Stuart's beggar," he said.

"Really? Where?"

"Heading into the church basement looked like."

Renata stared behind her at the *parroquia.* She seemed fascinated. And then she gave Atticus a fleeting glance and walked across to the police station and in Spanish explained who they were to a boy who'd looped and crossed canvas straps of cartridges over his pigeon chest. The boy gloomily heard Renata out and jigged his rifle sight toward the interior, and Renata and Atticus walked inside.

A jaunty man with the yellow stripes of a sergeant's rank was feeding on a banana as he sat at a wide mahogany desk in a room that was otherwise as open as a night-train depot. The green tile floor was unswept, gray cobwebs waggled in the air, and a hundred years of boot marks and spitting stained the green walls. An oranged map of Resurrección behind the desk was covered with Saran Wrap and pleated with tape. The jungle along the highway was roughed out with X's and with the words *Las Ruinas.* Renata told the sergeant their names and purpose in Spanish, and the police sergeant looked fully at Atticus like he was no more than fancy clothes he didn't want and fine boots that he did. He finally held out his hand. "We wish you visa."

Atticus found it in his wallet and the sergeant took his time spelling out the English words on it, then he folded up his banana peel before squeezing it into his pocket behind a name tag that read "Espinoza." His skin was a freckled, caramel brown, and there was only a faint hint of gray in his hair though he seemed to be in his sixties. While still focused on Atticus Cody's visa, he offered, "I have know your eh-son. We pass on the street, my mind take a picture."

133

Sergeant Espinoza handed the visa back and said, *"Siempre muy borracho."* Always very drunk.

Renata replied in irritated Spanish, and Espinoza sheepishly hunted through an upper drawer in the mahogany desk. When he'd got out a ring of old skeleton keys, he held a harsh policeman's stare on Atticus and asked, *"¿Está listo?"* Are you ready?

"Sí," Renata told him.

"You look not well," Espinoza said.

"Montezuma's revenge," Atticus said.

Espinoza seemed offended but got up and unlocked the iron-barred door and ambled down a hot, green hallway, his knuckles grazing against the walls. On the right was a foul dormitory as big as a gym, with just one door and four iron-barred windows high overhead and probably twelve prisoners on their hands and knees, wiping the floor around their green canvas cots with sopping towels that they twisted into tin pails. Espinoza stopped to insert an iron skeleton key in an old plank door with a hand-printed sign on it that read DEPÓSITO, and he let Renata and Atticus step past him into an overwhelmingly hot storage space that was as jammed as a pawnshop with assorted luggage and boxes and car tires and Mexican Army rifles and a Chevrolet V-8 engine. Espinoza worked himself down a skinny aisle, talking to Renata in Spanish. She translated, "They've got his gun and clothes and motorcycle and he has no idea what else." The sergeant got to a green paper package that he flung across the room like silage. "We're supposed to check it," Renata said.

Atticus squatted to tear the green paper away and saw Scott's frayed wallet, a Swiss watch just like his own, a worn, yellow chamois shirt, and the fly and side pocket of his paint-dotted blue jeans. Opening the wallet, Atticus found no *pesos,* but he did find a Mexican library card, a Bancomex card, a passport picture of Renata, an expired Visa credit card, and a torn slip of paper with phone numbers on it. His Colorado driver's license and American Express card were gone, just as Renata had said. Atticus thought about asking Espinoza about them but quickly imagined the sergeant's shrug, his feigned or real ignorance, and he didn't bother. Stolen, he guessed; he'd get Frank to cancel the credit card account. He fitted the wallet in his front pocket and laid a hand on the clothing. Even that wasn't right. Atticus had been inside the police station for less than ten minutes, but already his perspiration was beading up from his hands and wrists. His shirt was grayly spotted with it. And yet Scott had been wearing a hot yellow chamois shirt and blue jeans. Atticus picked up the yellow shirt and pressed it to his nose but could smell neither blood nor sweat nor turpentine nor paints.

Espinoza was heavily breathing over him, and

Atticus looked up to see in the policeman's hands the handsome twelve-gauge shotgun with its checkered walnut stock. Atticus stood up to cautiously accept the shotgun, and Espinoza spoke to Renata in Spanish.

"He says not to worry, they took the shells out."

"Shells?"

She seemed puzzled. "That's what he said."

"*¿Cuántos?*" Atticus asked Sergeant Espinoza and patted the shotgun's magazine.

Espinoza frowned and held up three fingers.

"*¿Donde están?*" Where are they?

Sergeant Espinoza shrugged.

Atticus turned to Renata. "You don't regularly put four shells in a gun if you're fixing to kill yourself. You figure one oughta do it, don't you?"

Renata just stared at him.

Espinoza was perusing an inventory sheet, and Atticus followed him past the Chevrolet engine to a nook where Scott's Harley-Davidson, with a film of dust on its fuel tank and jungle grass on one foot peg and handgrip, was angled over into the anarchy of five or six misshapen bicycles. The key was still in the ignition. Espinoza tried to lunge it over its kickstand, but the six hundred pounds tipped into him before Atticus jerked the huge weight of it upright and adjusted it on its kickstand again. He put the shotgun beside the green package of clothes as the police sergeant rummaged through a gray steel file cabinet and pulled out a red folder and handed it to him. Atticus sat in an oak chair and hooked on his gold-rimmed eyeglasses while Espinoza spoke in Spanish.

Renata said, "He says he had an assistant fill out the report for him. He was fishing for tarpon off the Gulf of Honduras."

Atticus looked up and out of habit asked, "You get anything?"

Espinoza smiled and held his stomach. *"Mareado,"* he said.

"Seasick," Renata said.

"Mareado. I'll have to remember that one." Atticus paged open the red folder to a form filled out in Spanish, which seemed to be Sergeant José-María Espinoza's report of his *investigación de suicidio.* The body was identified as Scott William Cody, a blue-eyed white male. His height was one meter ninety centimeters; his weight was eighty kilos. His *ciudadanía* was the United States; his birthplace Antelope, Colorado; his *residencia provisoria* was 69 Avenida del Mar in Resurrección. Whoever filled out the report was a gun fancier, for far greater detail went into its description: a four-foot-long Winchester Ranger SG twelve-gauge pump shotgun, model 1300, weighing seven and one-half pounds, with one fired Federal shell in the cham-

ber and three shells in a magazine that held five. Everything else seemed of far lesser import. Atticus could make out little more beyond Renata Isaacs's name and the hour the police arrived on the scene, *"las diez menos cinco,"* or 9:55 A.M. And that was it. It could have been the report of a household accident without injuries, of an American's favorite shotgun having been stolen.

Atticus flipped over the page and was aggrieved by a faulty, off-focus, black-and-white photo of the face he'd briefly seen in the coffin, flesh and sinews torn from the skull, the right eye just an ugly socket, the blond hair glossily matted in blood, and blood painting his jaw and neck, caking inside his right ear. Underneath that was another photograph taken from the front door without a flash so that Scott was just a faintly seen figure behind four unbusy policemen in the foreground. A high-angle photograph showed him sagged over in the green wingback chair with his first finger inside the trigger housing of the shotgun at his feet. Each photograph seemed to emphasize the head wound or the features of the room, so there was nothing to offer a father a painful, final glimpse of his son, he was just any human being in gradual decay. Atticus stared again at the high-angle photo. Scott's bare left foot listed over onto his ankle; his right foot was square to the floor, and a dark saucer of blood

and found the right place for it.

Renata said nothing as she gathered the green package of clothes. Atticus unhinged the shotgun and fitted it under the shock cords of the Harley-Davidson's saddle seat, and Espinoza held the door as Atticus pitched his hundred fifty pounds into the heavy motorcycle, rolling it down the green hallway. He fought the Harley onto the floor tiles of the lobby, and Espinoza and another policeman helped him brake and bump it down the front steps.

Hundreds were in the square and the *jardín* listening to the church plaza orchestra's guitars, violins, and trumpets play "Tú, Sólo Tú" as a seemingly famous old crooner in a green mariachi suit sang, *"Y por quererte olvidar me tiro a la borrachera y a la perdición."*

Renata stood on the sidewalk as Atticus got on the motorcycle. "Shall I go back home with you?" she asked.

"Nah."

Renata stared at him. With suspicion. "You're not too faint?"

"I'll be fine." Atticus handed her his Stetson and said, "Hold on to my hat for me, will ya?" He adjusted the spark retard underneath his right leg and jumped down on the kickstarter, jacking the throttle with his right hand until the tailpipe's black smoke grayed and the great engine's roughness calmed into gentle nickering sounds.

140

Renata was still staring at him, but with a difference, as if they'd harangued for a good while and he'd brought her around to his way of seeing things. "Was he murdered?" she asked.

"I think so."

Atticus clicked the Harley-Davidson into gear with his cowboy boot and jolted out into the street between cars, cruising along with the taxis and hotel rent-a-Jeeps until he happened onto Avenida de la Independencia, and from there on he knew his way and got up to speed on the gray highway into the jungle, sinking through fifty and sixty on the straightaways, just touching his age with the needle, the big engine crackling, the wind swelling out his cowboy shirt and swatting his gray hair awry. When he was far away from Resurrección, Atticus feared he'd missed the turnoff for Scott's workhouse, but then saw a teenaged girl in a lime green dress urging a gray zebu cow along the highway by tapping its flank with a bamboo pole, and just behind her a red flag was hanging from a tree. Atticus tilted over into a sharp turn to the east and into the green alley of weeds and overgrowth that was increasingly tinged with the salt and seaweed odors of the Caribbean.

And then he saw the bright savannah and just a glimpse of dark blue water and the green heave of grass and stone that was once a Mayan lookout on the sea. Atticus rode up to it as he presumed

Scott had, shut the motorcycle down, and ascended the high hill with the shotgun, practically on all fours, pausing halfway up to rest, and pausing again to rip the yellow police tape from the door before going inside.

Everything was just as it was on Saturday. Atticus sat in the green wingback chair pretty much as Scott had in the picture taken from the front door, tilting to his right and gingerly touching his fingers to the floor. If it *was* suicide, Scott would have been facing nothing as he killed himself there. Whereas he presumably slumped in that chair of a night and fixed his stare on a half-finished painting. Atticus got up and put the shotgun together and aligned it on the floor just as it was in the high-angled photograph. Sitting again, he got back into Scott's pose and, holding on to the shotgun's barrel with his left hand, brought it upright so that it was on its heel plate and the front bead was touching his face. And that felt wrong: his right hand was twisted inside the trigger housing and his forearm winged out from the shotgun's fore end. Atticus planted his right boot just where Scott's foot was in the pictures, and let the shotgun go. The fore end fell against his thigh and skidded forward into his groin. Atticus tried it again, inserting his right thumb inside the trigger guard just as he would if he were killing himself, and imagining the jolt of the shotgun blast so that he jounced back against the green chair. And the shotgun fell against his right thigh again.

But what if the gunshot didn't kill him immediately? What if he were there for an hour or so just bleeding? Conscious or unconscious? Half his face gone? Wracked in agony? Would he kick the gun away? Would he go for the gun again and try to finish it?

Atticus walked to the bathroom and held cold water to his face, his thoughts flying. Suppose he *was* murdered. Suppose Scott walked to the front door and was killed there and he was too heavy to lift. His killer would have kicked the green wingback chair around so it was angled toward the door and the haul would be shorter, easier. Which way would his blood flow? Like in the photograph, toward his ear for as long as he was on the floor. And the blood would have been telltale: if it stained the tail or back of his shirt, the killer would have to take it off and put another on him, get one from a hanger in the closet. Even pull off his shoes if bloodstains got on them. And if it was murder, the shotgun might have been stolen first and loaded with more than one shell. If it was murder, things began to fit together. If it was murder, Atticus thought, Scott's father would not feel so much at fault.

Closing up the studio, he walked out to the cliffside. Hard sunlight glanced off the seven blues of the Caribbean Sea, and a southerly wind lightly feathered the waves as they grew giant against the jutting limestone and loudly cracked apart. A purple and green network of sea-weed and kelp braided the white sand at least ten yards away from the gnarling white surf. Wild oleander was growing along the upper cliff and up there too was a small porch of flat rock that held, he was half sure, a shoe.

Atticus used the shotgun as a staff as he halt-ingly slipped down through greenery until he was on a gray lintel of stone. There he teetered along until he knelt on the flat rock and reached to get hold of the flung penny loafer. The shoe was cordovan brown and fairly new, the manufac-turer's name, Cole-Haan, still gold on the heel pad inside it, a faint trace of blood on its shank. He hunted the hillside and shore for the other shoe and found himself frowning down on the churning water where Renata sloshed up to the beach yesterday.

And then a general uneasiness caused him to gaze back up to the *casita,* and Atticus saw a human form seemingly glaring down at him, his skin color, his face, his height ghosted into mys-tery by the blinding, white sun just behind him. Atticus yelled, "Who's there?" and whoever it was took a few steps back and turned and hurtled out of sight.

Atticus thought about going after him, but the hill was too vertical and he was too weak and forest was too close to the house, so he skidded down the hillside and for some time sat on the hot motorcycle in frustration and fury and grief, and then he turned the ignition and gunned the engine with his right hand and let go of the clutch. The Harley-Davidson jerked up and jittered sideways over the weeds and then righted itself in a sprint to the highway.

Riding toward Resurrección, he passed a hamlet where a frail, filthy girl was squatting outside a shack of dry yellow palms and sticks, dourly pressing corn mush into tortillas as a gray old woman peered out at her from one of six hammocks in the sleeping room. And then there was a shop with a shaded porch where a boy in a stained cook's apron sold hot Coca-Colas and pregnant women tilted along the highway with big plastic buckets of water they'd filled at a spigot. Hungry dogs in twos and fours slinked away from human beings. Hens and roosters pecked at the earth. On a pale blue building was painted LONCHERIA, and inside were picnic tables where overweight men in dirty T-shirts were eating tamales and black beans and rice from white paper plates. Heaped on a countertop were cooked pork chops in an orange sauce. Black flies cruised and alighted and flew up again as an old woman lazily flapped a comic book over the pork.

Walking away from there was the teenaged girl

in the lime green dress he'd seen earlier, the bamboo pole still in her hand. She paused and earnestly stared at him as he slowed and walked the motorcycle around. A few yards beyond her the zebu cow was browsing through fume-stained grass that was as high as its hocks. Atticus rolled toward the girl and turned off the ignition and tilted into the motorcycle to rock it up onto its kickstand. He could hear the high whine of jungle insects and the trills and caws of birds in the lush green canopy overhead. She wore white ankle-high stockings and dark brown shoes. She was probably fourteen.

"Buenas tardes, señorita," he said.

"Buenas, señor." She nervously turned and walked alongside the cow, taking hold of one long ear as she tapped at its foreshank with the pole. The zebu ignored the girl and lowered its great head to some green weeds farther away. It pained the cattleman in him to see the zebu's ribs so plainly beneath its hide, but he helped the girl herd it by authoritatively slapping his hard palm on the zebu's sharp pinbone, and the cow hopped into a short jog, its full round udder swaying between its legs. Atticus joined the girl and the milk cow in their slow amble along the highway.

"Perdoneme, señorita. Yo soy el padre del señor Scott Cody."

The girl said nothing but gave him a haunted,

sidelong look as she again urged the cow with her bamboo pole.

"¿Sabe?" he asked. You know what I mean?

She gravely nodded. *"Cotzi."*

"Sí." To his wonderment he found the Spanish to go on. *"Mi hijo está muerto."* My son is dead. *"Miércoles."* Wednesday. *"En la noche."* In the night. *"¿Comprende?"* You understand?

Like a schoolgirl, she obediently glanced at him. *"Sí, señor. Lo siento."* I'm sorry.

Atticus pointed to the shotgun that was un-hinged into stock and barrel and wedged under shock cords on the motorcycle's saddle seat. *"¿Escuche la arma?"* You listen the gun?

Although she seemed puzzled, she responded. *"Sí, señor."*

Surprised, he asked, *"¿A qué hora?"* At what hour?

She shrugged and thought. *"A medianoche."* Midnight.

The zebu stopped with the certainty of a piano and tore away weeds that slowly rose up into its mouth with the sideways crunch of its jaws. The girl stared at Atticus as he struggled to find the vocabulary for his hundred questions and finally settled on *"¿Usted ver mi hijo temprano?"* You see my son early?

She spoke but he couldn't interpret what she said, and he made a hand signal for her to repeat herself. "What was that again?"

Shutting her eyes and pillowing her right cheek with folded hands, she rephrased what she'd said in a paragraph, saying something about her brother and sister and using the words *adormecido* and *coche*. Sleeping and car. They'd seen him sleeping in his car. *Motorcycle* in Spanish was lost to him, so Atticus pointed to it. *"¿No ése?"* Not that?

She half-smiled as if he were joking. Sleeping on a motorcycle. She shook her head.

Wondering aloud, he said, "Why were you there?"

"No comprendo inglés, señor."

Writing the sentence in his mind first, he tried, *"¿Por qué usted allí, señorita?"*

"Vimos las luces en la casita," she told him. We saw the lights in the house. *"A veces lo mirábamos pintando."* We sometimes watched him painting.

Atticus caught the gist of it but wasn't sure he'd heard right. Was Scott sleeping in his car while the lights were on in his house? Who'd turned them on then? And how could Renata have found the Volkswagen near the *jardín?* Atticus fought to put his confusion and perplexity into words, but his Spanish failed him, and he could tell the girl was hankering to go. *"Muchas gracias, señorita."*

"De nada," she said, and whacked the milk cow on its hindquarters until it walked ahead.

When he got to Scott's house on Avenida del Mar, he killed the Harley-Davidson's engine beside the front door and rocked the motorcycle up onto its kickstand. He felt about to faint as he walked inside the house, so he put the shotgun on the floor and fell back onto the sofa and shut his eyes and heeled off his hot cowboy boots. A tropical breeze found his face, as perfumed and soft as the hair of his wife in bed, and he turned to it and in the flush of fever saw the faded denim of the sky and the navy blue of the sea and the tall sliding door to the pool half open, letting the air conditioning out. His hand gripped the right arm of the sofa and he pulled himself to his feet, tottering a little as he walked to the terrace and rammed shut the wide glass door. And then he heard a soft, stitching noise that halted when he tried to find it. The house seemed to settle and he looked at the ceiling, feeling a presence in Scott's upstairs room. Even if only for a second, Atticus found himself thinking that Scott was alive up there and it all had been a fraud, a horrible mistake, a mean-spirited fiction that had misfired, and he wished it were so. "Anybody here?" he yelled.

Stillness.

His head reeled and he caught a dining room chair with his hand. Walking forward a little, he tilted feebly against a framed print on the living room wall and frowned at hushed whispering and the faint thud of a telephone receiver finding its home on the machine. "María?" he called. "Who's in the house?" Atticus went to the foot of the stairs and with both hands on the banister held himself upright as he fixed his gaze up through the well to the second floor. Harsh white sunshine on the hallway wall was blinked by shade, and then Atticus saw frayed blue jeans and Nike Air running shoes halt at the upper step. Even as he hoped, however, a hard dark brown hand took hold of the railing and a teenaged boy in a Dallas Cowboys jersey fumbled down the stairs with his head turned away and hidden behind his hand as if he feared a photograph would catch him in his shame.

Atticus shouted, "The *hell* you doing here? Huh?"

Hunching further down the stairs, the kid got to the landing and hung there, his pretty-boy face full of grief, as he figured out what to do next.

"Saw you at church yesterday. Didn't I? At the funeral?"

The kid seemed not to know English, but a hurtful thought seemed to writhe through him and he suddenly surged forward like a football blocker, his left shoulder slugging hard into Atticus, felling him, and then the kid hurried to the dining room and out onto the terrace where he scrabbled up onto the high wall and flung himself out of sight.

Easing his way up from the floor, Atticus felt the full anger and humiliation of old age, finding no fight or scare in himself, put hard on the floor by a petty thief who must have thought Scott's father would have gone home right after the funeral.

The dining room telephone rang and he went to it. "Hello?"

"How was it?" Stuart asked.

Atticus sorted through the things he might have meant by "it" and said, "The police station. Kinda grim. Renata didn't say?"

"I haven't seen the dear."

Stuart was an old-time exile in Mexico, he thought. Stuart had learnt not to know anything. Atticus told him, "We had an intruder here."

"Oh, *no!* Who?"

"Kid. Sixteen, seventeen years old. I got back and the pool door was open, and I heard him using the phone upstairs. His hands were empty, so I don't expect he swiped anything. Don't have my sea legs yet or I might of wrangled him downtown."

"Oh, I'm so sorry, Atticus! How perfectly awful! You must feel violated! We've been having so *much* of that lately."

"Well —"

"Shall I have the police out?"

"I haven't been that impressed with them so

far. Like as not they'd say he was guarding the house so no thieves could get in.''

Stuart was silent. Atticus heard the scritch of his lighter and the fizz of a fresh cigarette as he inhaled. Stuart said, "We do hope you'll still find a way to stop by for dinner. Even after our contretemps this morning.''

"Well, that's nice of you. As a matter of fact, I'm feeling kinda peckish.''

"Oh, good. Shall we pick you up?''

"You know what, Stuart? I think I'll have a nap and get changed and hike to your place. I haven't seen that much of the seaside yet and I'd kinda like to.''

Stuart gave him directions and failed to offer a good-bye before he hung up.

With the dining room telephone still in his hand, Atticus decided to try Frank's place in Colorado, but Marilyn told him Frank was giving a talk to a cattleman's association up in Sterling. She took the message about Scott's American Express card, and he gave her a no-fuss, facts-only version of the past few days before saying he was expected for dinner and he was enjoying the fine weather so much he might just stay for a bit.

Then he got out Scott's frayed brown wallet and flattened the folded slip of paper with phone numbers that he found in it. The first number he recognized as Stuart's, so he dialed the second, which had an "S." in front of it. After five rings a frazzled-sounding Mexican answered, flatly saying, *"El Alacrán,"* and Atticus heard the noise of some guy slamming down a leather cup of bar dice before he figured that *El Alacrán* was The Scorpion, and hung up. "P. I." got a telephone answering machine that told the business hours for Printers Inc. And the penciled "R." phone number was picked up in four rings, a hotel receptionist saying, *"Bueno, El Marinero."* And Atticus could think of nothing to say; all he could think was, *R.*

About twenty minutes before sundown he locked up the house and went down to the beach through the pool gate. The sea was in green turmoil, the waves as big as one-car garages. College girls with hardly anything on were still on the hotel cots in a brassy shine of baby oil, headphones playing, margaritas in their hands, their faces tilted up to a sun that was now behind them. A plump American woman was sitting in a palapa's shade, her skin patched scarlet with sunburn, her rose sunglasses raising up from a P. D. James paperback to linger on the old man in the gray mustache and gray cowboy boots who was falteringly stalking by. After the Maya Hotel was the El Presidente, the saltbox *casitas* of the Encanto condominiums, the Hotel Mexicana, the Marriott, and then a staircase of seagrass and silt took Atticus up over an aggregation of dark brown stone that looked like the high pier of a lighthouse that neglect or age had torn down. Going over it and onto a gray boardwalk down to the sand, Atticus stepped onto a quarter-mile of public beach still crowded with Mexican families. Heavy women in overwashed dresses were sitting up on higher land, talking intermittently as they cooked tortillas on iron grills or just gazed at baby girls who were happily patting the sand. Teenaged girls who were probably their daughters sat on top of a big concrete sewage pipe as though they were still in a public schoolyard, snickering and whispering and modestly putting their hands to their mouths when they blushed and pealed with laughter. Then Atticus was aware of a half-naked American in his late teens walking up beside him in gray San Antonio Spurs gym shorts, his skin a ginger brown, his hair as wild as a lion's mane, a green tattoo of a dagger and a green teardrop of blood just about where his heart ought to have been. The kid falsely smiled and in a soft Southern accent asked, "Say friend, would you happen to be able to maybe help me out?"

A handful of rings and studs glinted from his ears, and there was a kind of silver tack in his nose. "You need pliers?" Atticus asked.

But the kid was too far into his skit to listen. "You see, I'm fixin' to get out of this hole and

I'm just about five dollars shy of a bus ticket. Might you have something you could lend me?"

Some Mexican boys played volleyball on the sand in dirty polyester pants that were rolled up past their knees. Some young mothers were struggling out into the waves in dark brassieres and underthings that they were trying to conceal with white filmy shirts made transparent by the sea. A skinny hotel cook still in his red tennis shoes and checkered gray pants stood ankle deep with a one-year-old boy whom he'd happily swing into the air by his wrists so that the boy's toes skimmed along the water in the spikes and scribble of handwriting.

The kid was still beside Atticus. He asked the kid, "Where would you go?"

"Belize. Even Guatemala. Anywheres really. Heard good things about Costa Rica."

"You been living here for a while, have ya?"

"Two heathenish years if you count jail time. Which you oughta count triple."

Although he feared the answer, Atticus asked, "You happen to know Scott Cody by any chance?"

The kid's face was frankly stunned — *We know the same people!* The kid turned and walked backward as he perused the *playa,* looking past the hotels toward Scott's place but never quite finding it. "Scott lives up by the Maya some wheres." His hand flew out. "I used to remember but I'm too forgetful lately. Went to a bitchin' party there once. He's *wild.*"

Atticus heard the present tense but failed to correct the kid. One turquoise concession stand was selling green melon, cooked pork rinds, ginger brown bananas in a sugary stew, and black, barbecued chicken wings. A second concession that was crazily just a few yards away was under repair, and a boy in a bikini swimming suit was scooting along on his knees in the sand, painting at a huge square footage of green cement block with just a one-inch brush, turning a one-day job into many. On a stepladder inside, a man who was hidden from the chest up appeared to be rewiring palm thatching to the overhead poles, and a second man's only responsibility was to keep one foot on the lower step and to hand up eight-inch wires, one at a time. Atticus flipped open his braid wallet and licked his thumb to get out a five-dollar bill that he withheld from the kid, like he was teasing a pup. "If I wanted to find Scott or his friends, where would I best look?"

The kid frowned and hunkered a little as he raked back his sorrel-colored hair with a hand. "You police?"

"I'm his father."

The kid focused on his face. "Yeah! Right! In his house. You're the old man in that picture of his that he drew. My girlfriend thought you looked just like God."

was behind the heel.

Atticus frowned at Renata. "Shoeless," he said.

"¿Como?" Espinoza asked.

Renata fidgeted with the green package of clothes but found no shoes. She straightened. "Wasn't it possible Scott was barefoot?"

"Wouldn't of been on a motorcycle. And if he got out of 'em while he worked, we'd of found his shoes on the floor."

Offended, Sergeant Espinoza said, *"Ustedes hablan muy rápido."* You are speaking very fast.

Renata worriedly peered at the photograph, her hand tenderly finding his shoulder. Her face was so close to his that Atticus could see the fine blond hairs on her cheek. Even in that filthy room, he could smell her perfumed soap. "You're right," she said. "It is strange."

Espinoza was standing behind him, hissing out gray cigarette smoke and interestedly scowling over Atticus's head, as if seeing the photographs for the first time.

Atticus tapped them together and looked at Renata. "Three pictures?"

Renata spoke to Espinoza and he replied.

"Ran out of film," she said.

Atticus fumed as he handed the folder to him. *"¿Esto es todo?"* Is this all?

"Sí." Espinoza clamped it under his left arm as he flipped through files in a gray steel cabinet

Atticus put on a smile. "Well, our voices are the same."

"She was stoned of course."

"Hell yes," Atticus said, "goes without saying."

The kid looked at the five-dollar bill. "Wow, this is so television." And then he said, "Believe he hangs out in Boystown at night."

"Boystown."

"You know, massage parlors, whores, the after-hours places."

Atticus handed him the five-dollar bill. "You sell him a car by any chance?"

The kid hesitantly said, "Wasn't no warranty to it or nothin'."

"I know that. You have an accident in that Volkswagen you sold him?"

"No sir, I dint."

"Was there just the original equipment on it?"

"I think so." The kid furrowed his brow in a way that resembled profound contemplation. "Scott have an accident in it?"

"I think so."

The kid halted in his walk and hung there for a half a minute, then hurried back up the beach as if his five-dollar bill would be lost if he stayed. Atticus headed toward Stuart's villa on the cape, passing the pirate's den of The Scorpion, with its blue neon and its palm-thatched roof and wooden deck and its dock leading out to some tied-up speedboats that rocked and smacked on the waves. *Cerveza* bottles and plastic glasses with green wedges of lime still in them were tipped and scattered over sand that was as gray as cigarette ash. And then there were some private homes that had the spiritless look of failed financial investments, places not slept in nor enjoyed but kept up by gardeners and maids who turned on the burglar alarms at night and went home. And at land's end was Stuart's grand pink villa and Renata in a soft white glamorous dress and a shawl, facing west on the lush green lawn to watch the sun flame out.

Evening dinner conversation was full of Stuart and his qualms about the high-speed trains that might rape Resurrección someday, the shoddy plastic plumbing in the house that was now being fouled with rainwater, the fancy condominiums that were being sold at a loss with the peso in such pitiful shape. Stuart talked about his bookstore and *Publishers Weekly* and a female employee who intentionally got pregnant, and that fed other topics that were passed around like bowls of food and handily put down in favor of others. Everything was kept light and tittering, though there was something fraught about their talk, as if there were levels of meaning that a visitor to their household would only hopelessly try to interpret. Renata flattered Stuart or held her silence while

Stuart ruthlessly imitated friends or offered his firm opinions or quickly began arguments that were just as quickly forgotten. And Atticus turned his frosted glass of tonic water in his hand, imagining his son handling fall and winter nights like this, being as disquietingly quiet as he himself was, gently smiling at his company even while he fumed and ached inside.

He thought about the wrongness of much that he'd heard and seen in just two days. He considered asking Renata to go out and talk to the Mexican girl, but he felt unsure that he'd get anything further, that Renata was free to tell him the facts as she got them. Even now she was peculiar, flinching, private, scrutinizing, the first to start laughing, the first to stop, fairly timid in speech, tentative in action, for the most part seemingly uninterested in him. She was like a fresh, spoiled girl forced to eat with the old folks, and she couldn't wait for the dinner to end. Was he murdered? she'd asked, and he'd said, I think so, and she still hadn't asked him anything more.

Stuart finished the hollandaise sauce while delivering his assessment of the faltering real estate market, and Atticus questioned him about his own investments.

Renata said, with a hint of exasperation, "Stuart owns hotels."

"I have *partnerships* in hotels," he said, foolishly bowing to her. Stuart was falling into drunkenness, but he turned half around in his dining room chair and called, "Julia? *Más vino por favor.*"

Atticus filled his plate with fettucine. "Would it be likely I'd seen any of them?"

Stuart considered Atticus as if he'd found a fresh complexity in him. "It wouldn't speak well of your sterling character. They're in, how shall I say it?, a *sportif* part of our fair city."

"Would that be Boystown?"

"Unexplored depths, Renata!" Stuart said. She failed to smile at him. "Don't tell me you've been talking to taxi drivers?"

Atticus twisted fettucine on his fork. "I got big ears, is all."

"Don't think I haven't noticed," Stuart said, and tilted away as a plump, happy maid named Julia poured a Chilean red wine into his goblet. "Oh, *what* is the name of that one, Renata?"

"Which?"

"Barry helped me refinance it. You *know*."

"Casa Fantasía?"

"No, no, no! On El Camino, for god's sake!"

"El Marinero," she said.

Atticus held his face as it was.

"Yes! Exactly, darling. I blow you a kiss." Stuart held up the Chilean wine and frowned at its label, then put it down again. "Would you like to hear about my stroke of genius, Atticus?"

"Anytime."

"Wasn't it a stroke of genius, Renata? Would you for god's sake support me on *that?*"

Renata told Atticus, "Stuart advertised in the International *Herald-Tribune.*"

Stuart fell back in his chair. "Well, I don't have a story to tell now, do I? I have been *trumped.*"

"Oh, there's more to say."

"Well, that was the *punch line.*"

"Don't pout."

"*You* have been Madame Ennui all night, and then, when I have a good story to tell, you go and give him the punch line!"

"It's late," Atticus said. "I oughta be going."

Stuart held his wristwatch close to his face. "Ten o'clock is not late."

And so they retired to a green library for Kahlua and coffee, but the partying had gone out of them — Stuart was fighting off sleep and Renata's conversation seemed practiced, as though she were rising to an occasion; she finally walked over to a high bookcase and pulled down whatever came to hand, bleakly reading a paragraph or two before shelving the book again. Stuart politely asked Atticus dispirited questions about petroleum refineries and cattle ranching, frequently peeking at Renata as he lifted his fragile coffee cup until Atticus frankly looked at his own wristwatch and told Stuart what a good dinner it was and got up.

Renata laid her book aside. "Shall I drive you?"

"Don't bother yourself. I like to take a constitutional after dinner. Habit I picked up from Harry Truman."

Renata stared at him with fresh interest.

Stuart offered his hand but failed to rise from his chair. "I really must say, I am so *glad* you're feeling better."

"Thanks," he said, and took his hat from Renata, and went out through the front door.

"Vaya con Dios," he heard Stuart call.

Wind was herding a fold of clouds in from the Caribbean and was so cooling the night that he felt good about his suit jacket. His right stocking was wedging down in the heel of his boot as he walked up Avenida del Mar, so he hunkered on a bench in front of The Scorpion in order to tug the stocking high on his calf. And then he heard a radio being tuned and found a green and white taxi sitting among the hundred cars in The Scorpion's asphalt lot. And he gave in to his first impulse, standing up and hailing it with the shrill whistle with which he used to call Frank and Scotty into the house, and he got into the taxi even before it fully stopped. "We meet again," he said.

Panchito frowned into his rearview mirror. *"¿Cómo?"*

Atticus took off his Stetson. *"Señor Cody,"* he said.

To his surprise, Panchito seemed to have trouble placing him, as if he were just another gringo, but he grinned and said, "*Ay, sí!* Hello, my fren!"

"Are you the only taxi driver in Resurrección?"

Panchito laughed as though he understood, and then asked, "*¿Adónde?*"

"Boystown."

Panchito peeled around toward El Camino Real while he found a Mexico City station on his radio. A female voice was softly singing, "*Solo tu sombra fatal, sombra de mal, me sigue por dondequiera con ostinación.*" Looking over his shoulder, Panchito asked worriedly, "*Quiere una prostituta, señor?*"

Atticus shook his head.

Warning him, Panchito waggled his finger and grinned. "*Es peligroso.*"

"Everything's dangerous," Atticus said and fixed his gaze out the passenger window. The huge voice of the disk jockey seemed to be booming from inside a shower stall as he announced that the singer was Linda Ronstadt and the song was "Tú, Sólo Tú." You, only you. Within a few minutes they were far from the *centro* and heading toward fifty or more flashing neon signs of a kind of fourth-rate Reno. "*Por favor, pare en la proxima parada,*" Atticus said, and put far too much money in Panchito's hand.

Surprised, he asked, *"¿Quiere que espere?"* You want I wait?

"I'll be all right," Atticus said, but he wasn't sure. Hundreds of shamed and sullen men lurked outside the hotels and taverns, often withdrawing inside as if hauled in by a leash, or they tilted along the filthy street facing nothing but their own faces in the barred and blurry storefront windows. Every other building seemed to hold a cantina. La Cigarra. El Salón Carmelita. Texas. El Farolito. Waiting inside were forlorn young women sitting on bar stools and facing the front door, in fluffed and tinted hair and fancy polyester dresses that seemed fresh from some prom.

Houses had strings of drying garlic nailed up on them like holiday wreaths. Little children with gray, shaved heads and the red scars of body lice and razor nicks walked along with Atticus, talking beseechingly as they yanked at his clothing and lifted dirty, brown hands up for coins. Unhealthy, furious dogs were plunging along the flat building rooftops and raging down at the walkers. Woodsmoke and pork and kitchen odors were a taint in the air. Deep in a one-lane alley he saw a teenaged girl get out of her panties and hike up her skirt so a fat man still in his hotel clothes could heft her up by the thighs and force himself into her.

Atticus stepped around a girl kneeling on the sidewalk with a wooden platter of pork ribs and chili sauce and a scatter of flies like black peppers. An American man of his age passed by him in khakis and a plaid short-sleeved shirt, with the upright, serious, tottering stride of drunks who think they're handling drunkenness well. A fat young prostitute in skin-tight jeans sang a question to Atticus as she sashayed past. Halfway down the block a man in a powder blue suit petted his tie beneath the green neon sign for the El Marinero hotel. And in front of it was his son's old red Volkswagen. Renata walked from the hotel in a harried way and talked to the man in the powder blue suit. He shrugged in the full Latin manner, tilting his head and giving up his hands. And Renata was getting into the Volkswagen when Atticus heard high voices in a yell. And then a gunshot.

A hundred Mexicans in the street were hurrying toward the Bella Vista bar where gunsmoke was rolling gray and blue through the doorway. Atticus hesitated and then walked over to it as well, his hands in his pockets, *Don't mind me,* and found a dirty side window where he squeezed between some tiptoed children. Tatters and silks of gunsmoke still hung by the ceiling, and a quiet body was heaped on the floor as though it were only sandbags and clothing dropped from a great height. Blood flooded from his chest in the form of a leg, eddying across the plank flooring

165

and runneling fast between the floorboards. A handgun was still being held by an older Mexican as he howlingly sank over whomever it was he'd killed, but another man took the gun from him and the killer was free to hold the boy's face in his hands and talk to him plaintively and kiss him on the eyelids. Only then did Atticus realize that the body was that of the petty thief he'd found upstairs in the house, whom he'd seen at the funeral yesterday.

And then Renata was beside him. "Don't stay here," she said.

"Why?"

She took him by his elbow. "We have to leave now. I'll give you a ride."

She was silent until they were out of Boystown. "I was afraid you were heading here by the way you asked about it. And then your face betrayed you. Why the hotel, El Marinero?"

"You tell me."

"I figured it had something to do with Scott."

"The phone number was in his wallet."

"Uh *huh*," she said.

"You know anything about the shooting?"

A Mexican policeman held up traffic while an Econoline van from the hospital rushed past. Renata said, "That's business as usual these days, isn't it? If you have a gun it has to go off."

The policeman waved them ahead and Renata shifted to first gear and let out the clutch too fast.

The tires briefly screeched as the Volkswagen jumped forward.

"The kid," Atticus said. "I found him in Scott's house today."

She frowned at him in authentic surprise. *"Really?"*

"You wouldn't know about that."

She faced the street and seemed to force herself to go on. She was probably unaware she was silent until she'd gotten all the way to the house.

FIVE

You're wondering what woke you. A hand near his face; a hand that sought him but held back as if it feared being scalded. And then a faint whirring noise from the kitchen, on and then off. But there was nothing to see in the five o'clock gloom of the upstairs bedroom, and no hushed breathing, no hallway sounds, no feather of a human presence floating in the wake of a hasty withdrawal. And yet Atticus got up and hung there at the top of the stairs, wondering if he was imagining the faint smack of a foot on the dining room's pink cantera marble. After a while he walked into the room Renata slept in, flicking on the ceiling light and finding *Shakespeare's Plays* still there by the unmade bed and three empty Corona bottles on the floor.

Either Saturday morning or later Renata had retrieved her clothing and shoes from the walk-in closet but left behind the hard-sided green suitcase with its Mexicana Airlines luggage tag, the suitcase as *there* as a Spanish word suddenly remembered. *Escopeta.* Shotgun. Atticus pulled off the red shock cord and flipped open its hasps, finding inside just an old plastic bag from a shoe store in Nijmegen in the Netherlands. While he couldn't recall that his son was ever up there, Atticus was past being either sure or surprised. Seemed you didn't fully know Scott, ever; it was like trying to hold water in your hands.

His thoughts were too assailed for sleep, so Atticus got into his funeral shirt and his straight-leg blue jeans and boots. And he was finishing a bowl of cornflakes and milk in the kitchen when he saw the Radiola tape player up on the refrigerator and punched the rewind button. He put his bowl and spoon in the kitchen sink and filled the bowl with water, then he punched stop and frowned at the tape and forced down the play button. Atticus could see the right reel take up slack and heard Linda Ronstadt's strong and gorgeous voice singing a fiesta song, "La Charreada," holding a high note for what seemed an impossibly long time while the horns and strings of maríachis played behind her. Atticus went out to the seashore with the player cradled against his left forearm, his spirits lifting with the happiness of the music as he walked on the hard wet sand, heightening the volume as huge waves cracked and boomed like falling timber and the high winds flustered the palms on the roofs.

But as Linda Ronstadt was singing the first verses of a "Corrido de Cananea" she was abruptly cut off, and Atticus held the player to his ear to hear just a hushed ambient noise, of paint-brushes rattling and swishing in turpentine jars, of footsteps on a plank floor, as if one night in his studio Scott had mistakenly pressed record instead of play. Atticus hiked up a hillside of sand to get farther from the grumble of the sea and heard a spigot being turned and water gushing into a glass beaker of some kind. When the spigot was shut off, the water pipe briefly yelped, and then the beaker clanked down on the stovetop and there was the hiss and pop of a gas burner igniting. And then for a few minutes there wasn't a great deal to hear — he guessed his son was fiddling with the coffee and was too far away from the machine.

When he heard Scott walking out the front door and then heard nothing more, Atticus simply watched the reels turn, wailing for a further sound he knew would have to come. A flutter of unease troubled his stomach. His hands, he knew, would shake if he lifted them. The flint gray night was fading and the blood of sunrise floated in the east. Atticus looked at the fattening reel for a few minutes, and then he heard the front door of the *casita* open, and panting, and the sandpapering sounds of shoes in hard effort across the floor. And it was like the old days of radio theater when he was a kid, a few actors and a few sound effects and his mind flying at five hundred miles an hour. A fierce kicking noise was followed by the grief of the green wingback chair being skidded around on the planks. And he knew this was Wednesday night and he was hearing the murderer haul his son inside.

Atticus harbored a hate so huge he felt owned by it; he was afraid of what it might do. And then he imagined he heard the sounds for the ugly things he'd already seen in his mind, his son being heaved up into the green wingback chair, his feet and legs being arranged, the shotgun being stood upright on its stock and his hand being forced onto the trigger housing. Atticus got his handkerchief and pressed it hard against his eyes.

Exhaling heavily, he tilted his head close to the speaker, heard the murderer walk outside, and he flinched at the firing of the shotgun. Right after that he heard the faraway tattoo of fireworks. The fiesta. Hangers rang as Scott's blue jeans and yellow shirt were taken from the closet, and then there were the faint noises of clothing being changed: tugging and shuttling, the fall of an arm, the purr of a zipper, his shoes being taken off. The horror of it folded him forward, his face in his hands, his head nearly touching his knees, and then the player abruptly clunked off, the reel finished.

Atticus held his position, hardly breathing, fractured with pain, filled with straw. Was it harder to hear that his wife had been killed? This was a flood line so high on the house it would never be touched again.

Much later Atticus was grimly trudging along the hillside to the house when he saw an old Ford 150 pickup truck halted in the driveway. He put the Radiola on the refrigerator and peered out the kitchen window at an old Mexican gardener unlatching the gate of a truck bed that was filled with leaf blowers and mowers, bamboo rakes, and gunny-sacked bales of cut grass. Atticus walked outside and watched the gardener, who seemed not to mind that there was no talk between them, but merely hauled out a tray of what may have been pansies and knelt underneath a flow of pink bougainvillea on a high white boundary wall and furiously stabbed at the earth with his trowel.

Atticus guessed it was a quarter till eight. A listing white bus was in front of the Maya Hotel and a full shift of Mexican workers were getting out. A few doors down and across the street a spunky white bichon frise that he'd heard called Winslow was poking his nose in a hedge while a blond American woman in white jean shorts and an untucked man's shirt held sunglasses up to the morning.

The gardener walked forward on his hands and knees and got something from underneath the bougainvillea trunk. Sitting back, he held up and puzzlingly turned a used green shotgun shell. *"Un cartucho, señor,"* he said, and handed the three-inch Federal shell to Atticus as if it were merely an item of family embarrassment.

Atticus went inside and found the Winchester shotgun and fitted the shell inside the loading gate, then pumped the forearm on the magazine tube and watched the shell fly onto the floor. When you shot the gun, the shell stayed there, but it was lost when you filled the chamber again. Atticus stood in the hallway for a long time, imagining how it could have happened there, seeing his fallen son, the blood on the rug, an angry Spanish message scrawled in lipstick across the dining room mirror. He knew what he had to do. Atticus got the ignition key for the Harley and on a hunch got the Schlage key from the upper drawer in the kitchen counter, then locked up the house and rode Scott's motorcycle toward the pink spires of the *parroquia,* past the *jardín,* and, if he recalled correctly, four blocks down Cinco de Mayo. And there the pink mortuary was, the name "Cipiano" in big brass letters over two brass entrance doors that a janitor was polishing. Atticus braked and tilted onto one leg and yelled over his nickering engine, *"¿Abierto?"* Open?

The janitor offered only half a glance before saying, *"Cerrado."*

Atticus thought a moment and then accelerated

until Cipiano's was out of sight, then he angled over toward the shade beside a *tienda* where he killed the engine and knocked down the kickstand. Walking around the block, he found the alley Stuart had driven his station wagon along on Saturday and halfway down saw the dirt parking area behind the pink mortuary. And there he peeked through a green screen door into the still-dark interior, and he lightly tried the handle. A hook-and-eye lock held it closed, so he got out his penknife, snagged out the biggest blade, and forced the blade up between the frame and the door until the hook was tucked up above the iron rim of the eye and he could softly pull the green door free. Sagging into the hot stucco wall, he heeled off his boots and went inside.

The floor had been hosed down and he heard water trickling into a drain at his feet and elsewhere the soft chatter of talk on a radio, but under that he heard as well the faint purring of a fan behind a door to his left. He found the fan on a stool in a preparation room, blowing through a half-opened window the stink of human flesh in fast decay. Lying on a tin-topped dining room table was the corpse he expected to find there, a green plastic sheet tenting all but one foot. A beige luggage tag was wired around the big toe and on it was written "Renaldo Cruz." *R.,* Atticus thought. He held a handkerchief to his nose as he hoisted the green plastic sheet and, just as he thought he would, gazed at the faintly sallow face of the teenager he'd found at Scott's funeral and inside the house, his black hair now like weeds on his head, his frail eyelids weighted shut with peso coins, the heart wound from the handgun just a ragged black hole no bigger than his thumb. And he was so positive that Renaldo Cruz murdered his son that he wanted a hammer or crowbar to pound the kid with, anything iron and aggressive to swing into the pretty-boy face and angrily change it, to kill Renaldo again, kill him right. Avenging Scott was the only thing that any part of Atticus was saying; his rage was great enough that it took all the governance of his old age to keep him from hauling the kid off the table and kicking him in the head. But he cooled and finally pulled the green plastic sheet over Renaldo's face.

The kid had been naked. His clothing would be in a box or gunnysack in the room. Atticus gently tugged the high cabinet doors and gently nudged them shut, spying only chemicals and dyes and cosmetic paints until he came upon a green paper package tied with a string that he dropped down to the floor. He worked at the knot with his fingernails until the string loosened up, and he flattened the paper without rustling it. Renaldo's Dallas Cowboys jersey was stained and caked with blood and stank with too much use in the heat; his stiff blue jeans held the odor of sweat and dirt and urine; his Nike Air running shoes were size nine and orange with the earth you found in the jungle. Underneath the clothing was a plastic bag like those you put your fruits and vegetables in at the grocery store. And in it were some peso coins, a red pack of cinnamon chewing gum, a fine gold necklace with a crucifix on it, and a calfskin wallet, the paper money gone, no health or bank or credit cards, no Mexican driver's license, just a folded green receipt from Los Tres Hermanos auto body shop in Mérida and a Kodak color snapshot of a primped and pretty Mexican girl of sixteen or so in the plain white blouse and blue plaid dress of a high school uniform. She was sitting before a photographer's gray curtain with a faint, shy kink in her smile. Her fluid black eyes shone in the spotlights. Written in felt-tip pen on the back of the snapshot was: *"A Renaldo, para siempre, con amor sempiterno. Carmen."*

"To Renaldo, for always," Atticus said, "with love everlasting. Carmen." Looking again at the handwriting on the garage receipt, Atticus figured out that a fender and windshield were repaired and the fender painted, but one or all of the three *hermanos* forgot to note for whom and for what car. The job was finished on Monday of last week. Atticus grimly put things back as they were in the plastic bag, wrapped the green paper package, and hefted it up to where he'd found it.

The Mexican janitor walked in from the front of the building, a tin pail and a striped can of brass polish in one hand, a gray mop in the other. Atticus held the door open an inch and watched as the janitor skidded the pail on the floor, angled the dirty mop inside it, and turned up to high volume the box radio that had been quietly muttering Spanish. Attaching a hose to a hot water spigot, he twisted the tap on and gradually filled the pail, shaking a bathroom cleanser until it foamed, and then bending far over to sneeze.

Atticus walked silently behind him, and when the janitor sneezed again and went for his handkerchief, Atticus was pushing through the green door and out into the brilliant sunlight of the alley.

Then he rode the motorcycle out of town on the highway, hugging the middle of the tarmac to avoid farm people walking the hot pavement in their huaraches. But there was a winding in the highway and, in a flash, a little girl, right there in his lane, a full basket of limes balanced on top of her head. Atticus jerked hard to the left, but his speed was too great. His tires chirped on the tarmac and his locked back wheel screeched and the handlebars yanked at his right hand and wrist in the front wheel's try to wrench against the force of the highway. But then the motorcycle righted itself again and Atticus skidded around, his heart hammering, and watched the girl totter along, her frayed blue dress tilting at her knees and with nothing but the basket on her mind. *And that's how it happens,* he thought. *Sudden death.* Rolling past the highway memorials, his engine crackling in the heat, Atticus crept slowly enough to find a name or a date before he surged on to another. And then he found it. Crawling off the highway, he nudged the Harley-Davidson up to the freshly installed concrete cross with a heap of plastic funeral flowers at its foot. Chiseled into it was "Carmen Martinez." She was killed a little more than a week ago, on a Saturday. She was sixteen years old. *Con amor sempiterno.*

He went to Boystown. Walkers jumped away from the great snarl of the engine as he crept down El Camino Real between taxicabs and Ford rental cars and air-conditioned hotel vans filled with Americans who were probably trying to find bargains on hand-sewn rugs and nineteenth-century antiques before the heat got too bad. Right after he passed the American Bar and the Bella Vista, Atticus saw the *posada* up ahead and tilted into a hard turn down a side street, then took a left into a still-shaded alley until he arrived at a blue stuccoed wall where "El Marinero" was sloppily printed over a sprung and often-battered steel door. Atticus shut off the cycle and went inside, walking casually down the corridor to the front as four fair-haired and sunburned Europeans of college age huddled at the high front desk and heard one of their group speak Spanish to the cashier. Others slumped against huge backpacks on the tile floor, one blond woman braiding another's fine hair, a kid in filthy shorts and hiking boots abstractly twirling a finger in his here-and-there beard as he puzzled out a map. Atticus quietly passed through them and up the staircase, as confident as a paying guest who'd just gone out for coffee.

In the upstairs hallway he followed the numbered doors until he got to 13, where a plastic NO MOLESTAR sign hung from the brass-finished knob. Atticus lightly knocked on the door and put his ear to the wood. Hearing nothing, he fitted the Schlage key into the lock and gently turned the bolt from its home.

The havoc inside surprised him. Wonder bread going green with mold, hot bottles of Beck's beer and Coca-Cola, a torn-open sack of Oreo cookies, a hot plate and a case of Campbell's minestrone soup, a high stack of crime paperbacks in German, a box full of forty or fifty various sunglasses with peso price tags on them, an old-fashioned radio with a hanger antenna shinily dressed in aluminum foil, the floor littered with Kodak film cartons, and a tortured tuxedo shirt by Armani forgotten under a stuffed chair. A fourteen-inch neck, a thirty-inch sleeve. The plastic ashtray on the dresser was clean; there was no scent of cigarette smoke in the air.

Atticus looked into a closet and found no clothes, only a few hangers fallen to the floor, and the bathroom was free of personal articles, too, though there was a white stain of toothpaste beside the sink and a puff of four-inch blond hairs in the wastebasket, as if a brush had been cleaned. *A blond man,* he thought. He'd had it in his head that Renaldo Cruz had been hiding there.

Atticus petted the gray wings of his mustache with his hand as he sat on the bed and thought. Was there a connection between Renaldo and this guy? Why would his son have this phone number in his wallet? Was he putting a friend up here?

In frustration Atticus got up and tipped an ugly seascape away from the wall above the bed, but nothing was behind it. The fake wood vanity beside the bed was empty but for a Resurrección phone directory that was called a *guía de telefónica.* No Cody was listed in it, but when he backed up a page he saw Stuart Chandler's phone number circled in blue ink. He thought that strange. Paging ahead through the whole book, he saw only two other numbers circled, one for The Scorpion and one for a *farmacia* on Calle Hidalgo, the same pharmacy on the sales receipt for the cancer medicine. "Who are you?" he said aloud.

He went through the foods that were stored there but found nothing of interest. And then he went through the high stack of crime novels, hunting anything at all and finally finding in one the bookmark of a boarding pass on a Mexicana Airlines flight from Miami to Cancún, in the passenger name of Schmidt/Reinhardt.

Reinhardt Schmidt. Atticus walked over to the bed and heaved up the mattress with both hands. But finding nothing there, he let the mattress flop down again. And then he got down on all fours and frowned into the space beneath the box springs, and tugged out from between two boards a zippered plastic portfolio. He sat back on his heels to look inside it. A worn passport wallet held less than a hundred dollars in Deutsche marks, Swiss francs, and Dutch gulden, as well as an international driver's license that was missing its photograph and was issued in Rome in the name of Giuseppe Grassi. Tightly wrapped in a rubber band was a stack of nine expired credit cards in the names of John P. Gillespie, Jr., Joseph L. Naegele, Page Edwards, William Peatman. Either a forger or a thief. He fished inside a hotel envelope and held the trimmed negatives of two photographs up to window light. The first was a photograph of his son's Volkswagen on a highway at night, focusing on its taillights and framed license plate; the other was a photograph taken around noontime, of fender and front windshield damage to the VW, and behind it were other wrecked cars and a tin garage and a sign that read Los Tres Hermanos. Reinhardt crashed

Scott's car, was that it? Were Reinhardt and Renaldo in cahoots, or was that folded green garage receipt just something that Renaldo Cruz happened to get a hold of? And where was Reinhardt now?

Atticus walked around the bed, looked up the printed number for the front desk, and gambled by pressing 1 on the telephone and telling the Mexican woman who answered that he was Reinhardt Schmidt.

"Of course," she said, though he was probably just a hotel room to her. She had the English of a person who'd spent a while in the United States, but she'd adopted the Mexican politeness of pretending to know people and things that she didn't.

"You have any mail or messages for me?"

"Wait, please," she said, and a few seconds later told him with feigned regret, "There is nothing."

"Don't recall your name."

"Rosa."

"Right. Rosa, are you keeping a record of my phone calls?"

She seemed defensive when she answered, "Sure, always; for all our guests."

"Well, that's good because I forget: When was the last call I made?"

"You will wait," she said. Atticus pulled out his wallet and Scott's handwritten phone numbers, then sat with the paper on his thigh and unscrewed his fountain pen.

Rosa got back on. "Wednesday," she said. "Six o'clock."

"Would you be so kind as to tell me the number?"

She read it to him and he scanned the list for a match, finding none.

"Hate to ask this, but would you please give me that number again?" he asked, and he wrote it on the paper. Mexico City. "And before that?" he asked Rosa.

She sighed and said, "Same time," and she gave him the telephone number to Scott's house. "We have to charge even for less than a minute."

"Of course you do. And the other one was how long?"

"Four minute."

"I hate to trouble you further —"

"It is no trouble," Rosa said, plainly lying.

"Don't recollect if there were any other calls."

She seemed to scan a printout. *"Sí. Lunes."*

"Monday. Wonder if I could get that number, too?" She read it and he wrote it down. "Anything more?"

"Nada, señor."

Atticus suspected her Spanish meant she wanted their chat finished. He told her, "You see, I'm doing a little bookkeeping here, kind of double-checking my facts for my expense report."

"Por supuesto," she said. Of course. But a tone

183

of suspicion was filtering through.

"Exactly how many days have I been here?"

Rosa sighed.

"Don't count, just give me the date when I got here."

"December eighth, Mr. Schmidt. You don't remember?"

"Wasn't sure if it was that or the seventh," he said.

"I have business?" Rosa said, and after accepting his gratitude for her forbearance, she said good-bye and hung up.

Atticus lifted the half sheet of paper and looked at his handwriting. And then he dialed the first number Reinhardt had called. A female voice said, "*Bueno.* Cipiano."

"*¿Habla usted inglés?*"

"A little."

A half dozen things flew through his mind, but he remembered the call was made on *lunes.* "Would you be able to tell me if you had any wakes or funerals a week ago? Monday?"

"You are?"

"A friend of mine died," he said.

She sighed, but obliged him. A page was turned and she read, "Álvarez, Ellacuría, Hijuelos, Martínez, Ortiz."

"*Carmen* Martínez?"

She hesitated and got back to the page. *"Sí, señor."*

184

"Muchas gracias," he said, and hung up. Atticus dialed the Mexico City number just above Cipiano's. Wednesday, he remembered; four minutes. He heard a faint, official male voice — had he said American Embassy? Atticus plugged his right ear with a finger as he inquired, *"¿Quién es?"* Who is this?

The official heard his accent and asked him, *"¿Habla inglés?"*

"A little," he said.

A Brooklyn voice officially informed him, "You have the passport section."

Atticus stalled by saying, "I was afraid I had the wrong number."

"Your question?"

Wildly guessing, he asked, "Wondered if you had that passport ready for Scott Cody?"

"Was it Cody?"

"Really appreciate it."

"Hold on, sir," the man said.

Atticus waited half a minute.

"We do," the man said.

Atticus thanked the official and got off the phone. Was it Reinhardt who was flying to Germany? Was he trying to go there as his son for some reason? Had he hunted high and low in the house before he found out how to get another passport? Atticus got up from the bed, and then the phone rang insistently. *That'll be Rosa,* he thought. He held the zippered portfolio under his left arm as he locked the hotel room behind him. In the hallway he saw a heavy maid heave a white cart full of towels and bedding from a freight elevator, and he took it to the first floor, getting there just as Rosa was heading upstairs.

Then there was nothing to do but go back to the house. The front door was open for the fresh air, and María was furiously hammering an old-fashioned steam iron on handkerchiefs at the dining room table. *"Buenos días, señor,"* she said. *"¿Cómo está usted?"*

In English he told her, "I have no idea what's going on."

She smiled. *"Bueno."*

Exhausted, he got a Coca-Cola from the refrigerator and went out to the first-floor terrace. *What next?* he thought, and had no answer. A flock of seagulls fought and screeched over food thrown from the kitchen of the Maya. A hundred yards out a whining speedboat fanned right and spanked along the chop of a trawler, and farther out a freighter warped from view in the heat waves of the eastern horizon. Atticus thought of the choices Reinhardt would have if he wanted to hide out in Mexico: fishing boats, a tent in the forest, waterless shacks in the *barrio* you could rent for nine dollars a month.

Was the phone ringing? He stiffly turned, but the window glass offered nothing but a reflection of himself and what was behind him. He held the cold Coca-Cola can to his forehead. Kids were playing volleyball and running into the sea. White sailboats heeled in the wind farther north.

The pool door slid open. María was standing there with both hands on it. "*Teléfono, señor,*" she called.

Atticus went back inside and she tilted her head toward the flashing green light on the answering machine. "*Es urgente,*" she said.

Atticus got to it and pushed the rewind button, heard the reels spin to a halt, and pushed playback. Again he heard a soft, foreign, male voice saying, "*Hola,* Scott. Are you at the fiesta with Renata? Have a fantastic time —"

María shifted her ironing and frowned at a familiar voice on the machine. Reinhardt. Atticus hit the pause button. "*¿Lo conoce?*" You know him?

She flushed and said, "*Sí.*"

"*¿Cuál es su aspecto?*" What is his aspect?

"*Rubio.*" Blond. She thought further. "*Guapo.*" Handsome. "*Pero no me hace buena impresión.*" But she didn't like him.

He hunted the term for height. "*¿Cuál es su altura?*"

She shrugged. "*Como usted.*" Like you.

"*¿Usted lo ver aquí? ¿En la casa?*" You see him here? In the house?

"*Sí.*"

"¿Con mi hijo?" With my son?

"Una vez." Once.

"¿Sabe su nombre?" You know his name?

She must have thought she'd said too much. She folded a handkerchief.

Atticus hit the button again and Reinhardt went on, "I hate plays, plus in addition I have laundry to do. Don't worry, I have my own key. Shall we meet at the Bancomex at ten tomorrow?"

Wednesday night. The one-minute phone call from his hotel. Right after that was a tone, and Renata's voice saying, "Hey? If you're still around, we're having a cast party at Stuart's. Wanna come? See ya."

And then it was Stuart. At first he spoke a fluent Spanish that was intended for María, saying the message was urgent, and then he said in English, "We've had a spot of good fortune, Atticus. Your son Frank seems to have friends in high places. We've gotten permission to exhume and ship the remains. What luck. Shall I see you at the cemetery? Eleven o'clock. Awfully sorry about the rush."

It was then ten minutes till. Atticus hurried out of the house, got on the motorcycle again, and headed down the hill to the *centro.* But he wasn't certain where the cemetery was; he recalled that it was west of the *zona turística* and far into the *barrio,* but when he got onto El Camino he knew that was wrong, and he gave up on Avenida de la

188

Independencia after a few blocks. A giant super-market in a foreign part of the town had a public telephone outside. Atticus cruised the Harley-Davidson close to it, cut the engine, and rocked it up on its kickstand.

He was about to telephone Cipiano's when he saw Stuart's beggar outside the market with his hand full of coins, frontally confronting the shoppers and offering them his prayers. And Atticus was transfixed, because Stuart's beggar had on the gray Stanford T-shirt his son was wearing at Christmas.

Stuart's beggar caught sight of Atticus and for half a minute pretended he hadn't, his frank brown eyes trailing away from the cattleman's as he gave it some thought. Then Hector piously tilted forward on his crutches, heading toward the *centro,* his one *huarache* dragging the ground with a hushing sound. Atticus followed him from afar, strolling up Calle Veracruz a half a block behind him, past some gumball-colored shops, past a girl squatting by a red Radio Flyer, selling a wooden platter of pork ribs with hot chili sauce and the pepper of flies. A flock of sparrows flushed wildly out of a tree, then flew as one to a rooftop. Atticus watched a gray cat reach far down the tree trunk and softly fall to the earth and slink toward a hedge with its tail fluffed. Heat made the walk a job; there were side streets only one car wide that were without roof shade or breeze or human beings, where the scents were of woodstoves and slaughterhouses and the air seemed hotly physical. A butcher's shop, a *carnicería,* kept wild pigs on ropes in a side yard, and fowl were squawking inside a chicken coop. At the *lavandería* four women happily talked as they thrashed their sopping clothes on flat rocks. Atticus lost Hector just around a corner, and then caught up to him in the shade of a fortune-teller's green awning with lettering on it that said *Adivino.* And then he saw from a fresh angle the green laurel trees of the *jardín,* the six- and seven-year-old shoeshine boys, the Printers Inc bookstore, the *comisaría de policía,* the soaped American cars being rinsed with pump water.

Stuart's beggar was clobbering forward on his crutches around the side of the great parish church, past people sitting against its high walls and handrails with straw baskets for alms in their laps. Atticus then saw Hector tilted against the church and waiting for him beside a gray wooden door that he held open with his right hand. Atticus skeptically passed him and went inside, going down a ladder of ship's treads with his right hand sliding along the rail, and he stooped under the huge floor joists of the apse to peer into a huge, nighted cellar that was roomed into sleeping compartments, with green tarpaulins or the plastic that sofas are packaged in weighted to the floor with rocks. Great urns and pews and painted altar screens were stacked up in a gray velvet dust and a little girl in a dirty green dress was carrying water in a plastic bucket.

Entering the cellar, Atticus just missed a sleeping old grandmother curled up on some torn surplices, quietly tending her misery as if it were nothing more than a tired child. Beyond a junk-yard of one-legged chairs and wrought-iron candlesticks was a dark alley that the girl walked along until she got to a fat man on a four-wheeled dolly whose torso ended at his waist. Maybe twenty people were cloistered in that great cellar space. A pregnant girl crouched over a soup bowl and scooped up its sauce with a tortilla. Two frail old men with limbs like kindling lay on their serapes, playing dominoes.

Atticus frowned as he walked among them, his head turning right and left, looking for a further clue that would help him find the murderer of his son. And he stopped at a flattened cardboard box with the name Hotpoint on it. Whoever slept there kept a spiral notebook and pen beside the folded blanket that was his pillow. Atticus walked over to it and knelt there and flipped the pages to see a familiar handwriting.

And the light changed as though a window was blocked and he heard a voice say, "Will you forgive me?"

Atticus turned to see his son.

THE
HOUSE OF HE
WHO INVENTS
HIMSELF

SIX

Went native in Mexico for a while and made a friend of a shaman named Eduardo. Woke up coughing one morning in my shanty and found Eduardo inches away from my face and gently blowing cigar smoke at me. "Are you ready?" he asked in Spanish. And I looked out at three serious Mayans with wild black hair and filthy hand-sewn shirts that fell as far as their knees. Everything in them was saying how essential I was. So I walked behind them through a forest as green as Gauguin's Tahiti, honoring their habit of silence as we hooked off and onto paths seemingly without reason. We'd go ahead for half a mile and rest for five minutes, then hike for a hundred yards and rest for half an hour. It was impossible to predict when we'd stop, and harder still to tell how long the pause would be. I finally heard the boom and shush of the sea and held my hands up to shade my eyes from the flare of harsh sunshine and salt white sand. Finding the harbor was the whole point of the trip, but the Mayans halted again just inside the forest instead of going out to the water. I couldn't figure out their hesitation, and I asked Eduardo in Spanish why we were stopping. Eduardo looked at me like I was a toddler. And then he told me with infinite patience, "We are waiting for our spirits to catch up."

I have a flat board on my knees for a desk, and on it my Scribe spiral notebook — *Hecho en Mexico por Kimberly Clark* in Naucalpan — is opened to the first page. My pen is an "EF uni-ball Micro," with a fine point and blue ink. I have no idea whom I'm writing this for. We are waiting for our spirits to catch up.

I first met Reinhardt Schmidt just after I got back from Colorado. I was sane as Atticus then. And cool. Wearing shades and waltzing through the great open-air market in Resurrección. It was a hot and crowded tent city that was as loud as a kindergarten playground and filled with hard-up people selling handicrafts, fabulous fruits and vegetables, plucked chickens with the heads still attached, items fresh from the trash. You did not see many *norteamericanos* there, but you did find bargains of the hijacked, five-finger discount, *What the hell do I do with this?* kind: Gillette razors, Goodyear snow tires still wrapped in tan paper, floppy discs that sold for a nickel apiece, a guy in headphones sitting on the trunk of a green Chevrolet that held nothing but Salem cigarettes. Reinhardt called it his duty-free shop.

I felt a hand fall faint as a butterfly on my forearm, and I looked down at a kid holding up a bottle of Jameson's Irish whiskey while his other hand waited like a tray for his pesos. *"Aquí,"* he said. Here. And he was surprised when I told him nah. *"¡Es para usted!"* It is for Your Grace. And then he tried English. "We gave you our special price."

And then I heard a voice just beside me say as he handed the kid his pesos, "We seem to be the same person."

Reinhardt Schmidt did, in fact, look like me but was far more the kind of handsome, fine-boned, fashion-model blonde that seems fit to be a flight steward for Lufthansa. His age was forty or younger — he never said — but he was an inch or two shorter, fifteen pounds lighter, a fast-twitch, friendly, full-of-energy type in fancy sunglasses, a formal white tuxedo shirt with its sleeves folded high as his elbows, green fatigue trousers from some foreign legion, and feet that were miserably without shoes but did have ankle bracelets. A hand-sized flash camera was hanging from a frayed cord around his neck.

The kid took a moment to look from face to face, as if he was flummoxed, and then to touch his own hair in explanation. *"Rubio,"* he said.

Reinhardt looked at me and I translated, "Blond." And then I told the kid, *"Mi gemelo*

197

malvado.'' My evil twin.

The kid smiled and handed Reinhardt the whiskey and then hurried to his father's booth.

We introduced ourselves and we talked for five or ten minutes, no more. Reinhardt told me he was from Germany, but his English was the highly schooled kind that you hear all over Europe now and I figured that Germany was his geography of convenience, the origin of a passport he got by on. Even then I guessed he was lying, just another guy in Mexico on the lam; there was that wise-guy shiftiness, that hustle of flattery and fearing offense, of sizing you up for the squeeze while trying too hard to be friends. You saw his kind in all the American bars — hard-drinking, no-luck, full-time liars fleeing some trouble that was not at all glamorous, financial reversals in the restaurant business or one too many wives, but who forced themselves to confide that they were in Mexico on an inheritance, here to write a novel that four or five editors were definitely interested in, or hiding out in a witness protection program, for Chrissake don't tell anybody. You heard them out if only to know what topics not to bring up again and the true story became a whiff of unpleasantness underneath all that perfume.

I have few other recollections of our first meeting but that he pronounced *have* like *haff* and *situation* without the *chu* sound of American

English. Reinhardt told me if I needed a haircut — and his squinnying look said I did — he was the guy for me; he'd handled the heads of fabulously wealthy women in Hawaii — he hinted at a flair for other things, too — before he lost his work permit and took a galley job on Mick Jagger's yacht — a great guy, by the way — and happened onto a fabulously wealthy surgeon and his wife who needed Reinhardt to crew for them. A half year he was with them, sailing, playing backgammon, attending to their needs. Everything blew up a few weeks ago in Cuba — hot sex, discovery, gunplay — and he'd hightailed it here on the proceeds of the wife's Piaget watch, which he'd hocked for just such an emergency.

Well, he probably knew about the American expatriate's tolerance for bullshit and I, of course, have a further tolerance for madness, so I forgave his fabrications and when, hardly five hours later, Reinhardt bumped into me at The Scorpion ("Oh, hi!" he said. "Are you following me?"), we talked like friends in the making. I was fully medicated with gin and tonics by then and fell into a fraught stream of consciousness about Renata, an hour or more of she-done-me-wrong in forty variations, and Reinhardt took it all in oh-so-sympathetically, but fishing a little, too: Was she pretty? Did I have a picture of her? How often did I see her? Was she dating other men? Did she have a private income? And where did she live? I have forgotten my answers; I have not forgotten that I finally felt party to one of those *Strangers on a Train* routines; I half expected some unholy pact to follow when he halted his questions long enough to order a shot of José Cuervo and quaff it fast and peer resolutely into The Scorpion's mirror. But he just looked at me dully and said, "I have no money to pay for the tequila. Would you let me cut your hair?"

And so it was that Reinhardt arrived at my house one noon in the first week of January with his things in a kind of European saddlebag slung over his left shoulder. And I sat on a kitchen stool, a skirt of fabric under my chin, his silence behind me only increasing as his hands firmly held my hair and his scissors flashed, and I felt his tension for the first time and inferred that he was homosexual and hesitating over an invitation. But just as I was about to talk about what I fancied was not being said, Reinhardt filibustered about his jail time in Honolulu for hashish smuggling. A brutal year, but he made friends with a guy inside who got him a hairdresser's job with Universal Television. I forget all the ways in which he altered his first version of his life, forget even how he ended up with a film unit manager's job on four music videos, but a friend at Tri-Star liked his work so much that he was sent to Mexico to scout locations for a famous actress's next picture ("You haff heard of her, belief me") and then his boss went over to Paramount and the picture was put into turnaround and Reinhardt was left here high and dry. Which is why he carried a camera with him; he was always framing shots. Alan Pakula called him here just a few days ago and told him to sit tight, he was in preproduction on a film that would have a four-day shoot in Cancún and he wanted Reinhardt on his team. "And so I wait."

I was famished for English at the time and fairly indifferent to those florid tall tales, so I offered him feeble amens through all the foregoing ("Wow." "Too bad." "Amazing." "No!"), but as he put a gel on my hair, he turned his attention to me. Was I here on an inheritance? Was my father rich? Were my paintings selling well enough to afford a house like this? Oh, was I renting? Were the owners here often? Were the house and its contents fully insured? Reinhardt had seen a friend lose everything; he was just fantastically worried about me, he didn't know why. Well, he did. Don't be offended, but I seemed a wunderkind, even at forty. Which is why I ought to have worldly people to watch over my affairs. "You are so honest and trusting and others, I can tell you, are so . . . I have not the word: *schlau?*"

"Sly?"

"Yes! Sly. You do not realize. I have no talent

myself, but I have *skills.* You know? You maybe need help with the finances? Business affairs? Finding things at the cheapest price? I have contacts. And abilities. Arranging things is my gift."

"Here. Hold my wallet for me," I said.

Reinhardt smiled and flicked off the hair dryer. "Excuse me?"

His scheming was so obvious, so insultingly free of finesse and bunco, that I fell into silence. And then he held a mirror up and held his face close to mine so that both of us were in the frame. "Great haircut," I said. And it was true; just like his.

"Look at us," he said. "We could be brothers."

"I have one already."

Reinhardt casually turned to put the mirror on the kitchen countertop. "Oh? And what is his name?"

"Frank."

"And is he living in Colorado?"

But I was heading upstairs by then. I got thirty dollars in pesos and heard him fool with the Sinatra CD on the dining room player until he found "Witchcraft." And when I got downstairs he was hunting through the full rack of discs.

"Are you casing the joint?"

Reinhardt smiled uneasily. "What does it mean, 'casing'?"

I handed him the pesos and he stuffed them in his front pocket with only a furtive count. "Was it expensive," he asked, "this stereo system?"

Weeks hence, I feared, I'd return from my night work in the jungle and everything in that house would be gone, presto chango, and Reinhardt would be showing his kindness to some other wunderkind. "I have something I'd like to give you," I said.

"Oh?" he asked, and there was a child's Christmas glimmer in his eyes as I went to the hallway closet and hauled out a fair painting I'd fired off of a hillside and rainstorm skies and the seething gray waters just below my studio. I was frankly surprised by the honest respect he offered that sketch, the fascination and honor and joy Reinhardt took in holding it up and fully appraising it. You'd have thought it was a Corot. "This is fantastic!" he said. "This is great!" And there was a faint gloss of tears in his eyes as he fetchingly grinned at me. "We Europeans take friendship seriously. I'll have to do something for you."

Eight years ago at an East Village party I locked on to a psychologist who was researching a book on "thereness," as she called it, the high feeling some people have after going to a geography far from home and finding a *here is where I was meant to be* that they'd never felt before, as if the function of their lives was the bringing them to that place. I felt that way when I first got

203

to Resurrección, but initially thought it was just because Renata was there. But she was lost to me then, I knew that. I would telephone Stuart's villa and Stuart would be the first one to it, a husk in his voice as he asked, just to annoy me, "And whom shall I say is calling?" Envy and rivalry for Renata's affections were turning our meetings into skirmishes and our retreats into siegecraft and intrigues. Stuart told me once, "You'll be the ruin of her," as if I were a hooligan trampling the flower of Renata's reputation, and Stuart treated me in other ways like a frat boy and lout, like a fired employee. He pitied me openly at parties, he put up with me as one does a chronic pain, he once cleared our places after a dinner and pitched my cutlery into the trash.

Elated when Renata was with me, sick with despair and emptiness when she was away, I was powerless in the relationship, and she played with that just as I probably would have in the same position. Renata slept with me for old time's sake or out of inchoate spite for Stuart or in the hell-with-it spirit of a high school girl grown tired of the heavy struggles in the car. We did not do ourselves proud, Renata and I, and she came to the house one afternoon looking sleepless and forlorn and cried-out, and she told me, "I just can't do this anymore."

But she did do that anymore. We were both completely dependable in our irresponsibility.

Whenever Stuart was away, I hurried over to the villa in order to sit in palapa shade with Renata and piña coladas, our knees just touching, holding my stare on a bead of sweat as it trickled down her side and I thought *Oh, lucky droplet!,* and being gradually destroyed by the soft caress of her voice. Each sentence burnished and fathomable. The hour or two would have to end for some reason having to do with Stuart and we'd kiss and hold each other's misery to ourselves and my hands would find the old familiar places until she pushed me away.

Hardly a week before I went up to Colorado for the holidays I called her, my stomach flipping and my throat tightening with worry, wrapping myself inside the phone cord like a sitcom simpleton, and I tried to fix where I was in our emotional geography, fully unbuttoning my chest and informing Renata I felt like an inflamed teenager just born into the world of romance, *No one has ever loved like this,* and I was frustrated that there was no other way of putting it but to say again that I really really really loved her, had always loved her, as she knew, and the only future with any solace or purity or meaning for me was one with Renata in it: Would she fly up to Colorado with me? And then could we get married?

Renata sighed like the slow drag of a razor blade and said, "Ohhh, Scott . . . ," four beats at least to that phrase, four hammer blows to the spike I'd held to my fluttering heart. She told me she didn't trust herself with commitment, she felt too much turbulence just then, she didn't know if she was right for me, why didn't I try to find somebody else?

I was boyish with embarrassment. Awkward as a box full of shoes. Half-afraid I'd choke up or my shaky voice would crack, I hurriedly put up the fences and told her, "Well, there's no pressure. I just wanted some clarity, to find out what was real."

She said, "I think this is the reality we've heard so much about."

"Well, that's why I needed to say it. Everything gets to be Las Vegas after a while."

She told me prettily, "Don't feel rejected."

"If you say so." The phone seemed to weigh a hundred pounds. Silt seemed to be funneling from my head to my feet.

"We can stay friends, can't we?"

We'd both gone to high school, apparently. "Oh sure," I said. "Hell yes. I'd hate not seeing you at all."

"Stuart's here," she then whispered, and hung up.

On good days I painted in the jungle, faking it mostly, far too much hard-won technique and far too little imagination. Otherwise I hung out at the hotels, half-baked on hashish or the hard drugs I could score off college kids on their getaway flings, as goofy as that, cruising the *playa* in jams and sunglasses and a teal satin shirt, like the playboy of the Caribbean, hunting babes who were already high and inviting them home for an up-all-night, and then coming to in that *Oh, Jesus* chaos of emptied bottles and passed-out strangers and somebody softly sobbing upstairs. Anything to stay buzzed, to forget my obsession: self-prescribing Dexedrine, Percodan, Ritalin, and Valium at the *farmacia* and trying out fancy chemistry projects until I felt the attack of the thousand spiders. I was halfway through an imitation of Malcolm Lowry in Cuernavaca: fit and tanned in the afternoon, ginning for the camera in white shorts and huaraches, with Ovid's *Metamorphoses* in one hand and a full bottle of gin in the other; and far far gone by nighttime — feckless, sulking, furious, unshaved, in a fuddle of shame and neediness, failure becoming his full-time job.

But as skin-your-nose low as I was, there were a hundred others just like me down there, the formerly talented, the formerly with-it, hulking over shot glasses in the frown of drunkenness, not talking because we couldn't form words, having no company but fear, and pitifully tilting down for a taste because our hands weren't working quite right. You could find us haunting the *centro* at five A.M., walking car wrecks and homicides, waiting for the cantinas to open again and looking away from each other because we hated seeing that face in the mirror. You heard all kinds of reasons for being in the tropics: for their arthritis, their pensions, the fishing, the tranquil and easygoing ways, but the fact was a lot of us stayed because Mexico treated us like children, indulging our laziness, shrugging at our foolishness, and generally offering the silence and tolerance of a good butler helping the blotto Lord What-a-waste to his room. In high school my brother knowingly told me, as a kind of dire warning, "There are people who do on a regular basis things you have never even imagined!" I was now one of those people. Eventually it had become fairly ordinary for me to lose the handle and black out so far from home it might as well have been Cleveland, sitting there in a foul doorway in the *barrio,* fairly sure I'd had sex but not knowing with whom, blood on my shirt front, puke on my shoes, kids stealing the change from my pockets, and so little idea where my Volkswagen was that I used up an afternoon in a taxi just prowling the streets until I found it. And then, of course, there was a celebration and I fell into a wander again.

I have trouble putting a date to that particular spree, but it was late January, four months since I'd got off lithium, and for days I'd been floor-boarding it into what Renata used to call "a heightened state of mental fragility." Whether it was insanity or the aftereffects of pharmacy, I felt brilliant, ebullient, invulnerable, full of gaiety and false good health and a giddy, *Wow, isn't this freaky?* excitement. Well-being for me, though, is often like the aura that precedes the seizures of epilepsy, and I was headed for doom even while I was heartily being in my prime, Captain Electric, happy-go-lucky Scott. Stuart tried abiding me at Printers Inc and found himself not up to the task, and when I showed up at his villa ("Hi, honey; I'm home!") Renata gave me that *Oh, you poor puppy* look. We finally went out to inflict ourselves upon Mexico and found our way onto a bus tour of Resurrección, one of those *You are here* jaunts put on by the grand resort hotels to lure their elderly out of their rooms. And by then I was falling into a funk of aloneness and loss and desolation, hunkered down inside those old, old feelings of lunacy and finding familiar faces in all the Americans on that air-conditioned tour bus ("We know each other!"), as if I were part of some cosmic class reunion, déjà vu to the max — that old guy daubing sunblock fifteen on his nose and the hunchbacked woman holding her purse with both hands were as friendly to me as regulars at the truck stop cafe in Antelope, and wasn't that Aunt Claire? Were I still full of optimism and hail-fellow-well-met I would have been tempted to shout hellos and harass the old people with my frantic happiness, but my fluky head chemistry was forcing me into a bleak house of paranoia, restlessness, even terror, and I was trying to hold back, quiet the hectic tattoo of my heartbeat, put the watchdog out on his chain in case things got too weird.

Which they did. We'd motored through the *centro,* found photo opportunities with the fishing boats and the fruit sellers, heard the chamber of commerce pitch about a sky's-the-limit real estate future, and halted in front of the Church of the Resurrection. We were going on a walking tour, the girl in charge said. She said we would "find inside the *parroquia* many furnishing from Espain that the padres are bringing to Mexico in the eighteen century."

I have no idea if it was intuition or if some psychic floodwaters were opened and feeding me insights into the past, but I felt superior to whatever that girl's presentation would be. I felt like a former inhabitant, like I knew that place when the paint was still fresh, as if the hallways, the hidden doors, the shellacked pictures on the walls were as familiar to me as my father's house, and I'd forsaken the right or possibility of going inside again. Call it superstition or just a bad trip, but it felt as heavy as shot-in-the-night reality, like I was a kid on the first porch step of a haunted house, and my first remedy of choice was to hide my head underneath the sheets. I have a hard time making these events obey anything but the horrible logic of nightmare. I just know that as the old people herded off the bus I was shaded by the wings of madness and just sat there in my place, heartsick, holes for eyes, frail as an invalid, and shaking like it was forty below.

I heard Renata ask, "Are you spooked?" And I realized that she and I were the only passengers still on the bus, and that the frustrated driver was fixing a hard squint on us in his rearview mirror.

I just said, "I'm not ready for this."

"You don't have to go in," she said.

"Are you sure?"

"I'll see if you can stay." Renata gallantly went forward to help out the crazy person.

I heard Spanish and hours seemed to pass as I hunched forward, my face hidden in my hands, and inhaled, exhaled, as if that would be my only job from then on. Then I heard Renata say it was not possible, it was break time and the bus was being shut down, I'd fry inside with the air off. She took hold of my wrist and led me like a child to the door and ever so tenderly onto the sidewalk.

You'd have thought I was a head-on collision the way the Americans lurked on the sidewalk, talking about me, retreating, *Don't get anything on me* in their looks as I was hurried across the street, my feeble shoes shuffling a sandpaper rasp from the cobbled paving, and was settled like an ill-wrapped package on a park bench in the *jardín.* She said, "You know, I'm not that healthy myself. We can't take care of each other." If I looked at Renata then it was fleetingly, but I followed her with a toys-in-the-attic stare as she waded back into that hushed crowd, and I fended off self-doubt by thinking that this helplessness and despair was her scene, not mine, I was *fine* until she took my hand. *I have to go now,* I thought. *I have to wash. I'll eat my food with a fork.*

A full day later in my house and I was fine again, honest, no fooling. Waking up and holding my hands out in front of my face in that *how-many-fingers* final exam of full consciousness and perspective. But one frightening leer from Mr. Hyde in the bathroom mirror told me that I ought to get out of town for a while. And so I hurried into a bleached shirt and chinos and hiking boots, filled a box with food, block-lettered a note for María, and headed out to Eduardo's to hie the lunatic into the hills.

We shared a past, Eduardo and I, that made his friends consider my visits to his shanty in the jungle a kind of jubilee of wild invention, so within the next few days all the families in the area found their way to his place to hear the holy fool. My first night there fourteen men and boys settled on their haunches around a fire, inhaling huge handmade cigars until they were wholly intoxicated, and fascinatedly watched the zoo animal in his own private *Weltschmerz*. Eduardo finally squatted next to me and whispered in Spanish, "We wait for a speech."

I gave it some thought and recited in English a high school lesson of the first paragraph from *Moby Dick*: " 'Whenever I find myself growing grim about the mouth; whenever it is a damp, drizzly November in my soul; whenever I find myself involuntarily pausing before coffin warehouses, and bringing up the rear of every funeral I meet, and especially whenever my hypos get such an upper hand of me that it requires a strong moral principle to prevent me from deliberately stepping into the street and methodically knocking people's hats off — then I account it high time to get to the sea as soon as I can.' "

I have no idea what my English sounded like to them, but when I finished, a few softly applauded me in their flat-palmed way and one at a time they got up and finally left, fully entertained.

Hectic that life was not. We fetched water from the hole and used posts to tamp kernels of corn in a field that was still hot with soot and ash, but otherwise the hours passed at half-speed in a whine of insects, Eduardo instructing his heedless wives in their work while the heat soaked the black-and-blues away. Each night Eduardo's oldest wife, Koh, offered me a hideous brew of *balche* and chewed roots and seed pods that I took in perfect obedience. And I'd sleep hard, hammered, until high noon, hearing nothing but pigs and chickens and the chinking noise of machetes hacking down great trees in the jungle, feeling nothing but the infrequent, faint, floating touch of children's hands on my face and hair.

And then Saturday afternoon Eduardo and three of his friends invited me fishing, and we hiked through the forest to a harbor where a high-sided skiff was lolling on the swells as a teenaged boy in a racing suit fiddled with a fifty-horsepower outboard motor terribly hitched to its transom. I looked north and found far off the shell gray of the pollution that tarnished Resurrección, but the shoreline was otherwise foreign to me.

We got naked and thrashed out to the skiff with our clothes held high overhead, and I heard only highly accented Mayan as they pulled themselves up over the gunwale and joshed about something having to do with the gringo. I played the fifth wheel, *Oh don't mind me,* and faced them stonily from the forward sailing thwart as the kid in the racing suit got the motor going and we surged a half-mile farther out to a barrier reef where the water was as tepid and clear as Perrier but from a distance had the turquoise color of kitchens in the fifties.

The kid killed the motor and hurled overboard three concrete blocks that were tied to the painter line. An old face mask half eaten with salt and fairly good fins were handed to me, and then a four-foot spear just like they had. Winking, I gave them the old thumbs-up — what a good sport, what a trouper. The first to jump over the side was me, and then I heard hoots and the four crashing in, handling the seawater without face masks or fins and twisting like otters around the white elkhorn coral and infant sponges as they hunted brilliant wrasse and groupers and rainbow parrotfish. I went up for air a full minute before one of them did — they held their breath like turtles — but finally they all did flutter up for air with a boxfish that trailed shreds of blood, and I skimmed down past colonies of intricate lavender and red coral through a school of glorious blue tang that shuddered and broke apart at my presence and then rejoined into one mind again, and then I stroked farther past a terrace of black brain coral and sea anemone to a floor of sand. And there I found a stingray almost fully hidden in the sand, its fake-seeming yellow eyes flashing uninteresting news until irritation or fright finally registered and with a fluff of its gorgeous iron gray wings the sand floated away like smoke and the stingray was suddenly in a flight that was fluent as ointment. The first surge took it twenty feet from me, and then in its sovereignty it glided into a stall and oh so gently rippled its wings until the floor settled over it again.

Either I read it somewhere or Eduardo told me, but in their religious ceremonies ages ago, pre-Cortez, the Mayan high priests used to stab the barb of the stingray's tail in their penises and the poison would kick them into head trips that seemed to offer hallucinatory interpretations of the future. You'll have a sense of how far gone I was then that I found the hurt and danger of that kind of rush crazily alluring. I got high on threat and foreboding; I was like those heroin addicts who find they can get off just with the needle. I ought to have flashed up to the surface for air, but I felt a strong and irrational need to touch that stingray, and I kicked down until I was just above the fish, watching it blankly watch me.

I have given up trying to be persuasive about this. You get these looks: *Oh sure, stingrays.* But in fact a flock or herd or plague of stingrays majestically soared in from nowhere, five or six of them wrestling up against me in a thrall of motion, their soft wings sheathing me, their tails frantically whipping, falling away only to flare up against my flesh, showing their white undersides as their toothless mouths seemed to foolishly smile. I have no idea what attracted them. I have never felt anything so much like pure muscle, that filled me with such loathing. It was like one of those Renaissance paintings of Saint Anthony being persecuted by demons. The stingrays jolted hard into me and held me under and one blunt head knocked my face mask off. And I was near fainting for lack of air when I heard the Mayans there with me, churning their legs and fighting the wings until a spear jarred into one and a pink orchid of blood seemed to grow from its skin and their hands took hold of its head and ventral gills. And as I shot upward, they gingerly followed, hauling the fish to the skiff.

The kid was kneeling by a gunwale with a gaff. Enormously pleased, he helped me up into the boat and patted my head and heaped Spanish praise on me until he could heave the stingray onto the flooring. But then the others got in and huddled far from me by the engine as if they were afraid of getting anything of me on them. Even Eduardo found nothing more to do than frown at my bad karma.

We went farther up the coast to an inlet and the pretty white skirt of beach that was near Eduardo's shanty. Women in five-dollar American dresses were there chanting songs as they husked corn around a fire, and Eduardo's wife Koh shyly handed me a jar of the fermented corn whiskey called *chicha.*

I frankly brought nothing to that party; I was an anchorite, *il penseroso,* off by himself on a rock, hearing their talk but not understanding, hearing the high whine of insects at sundown. I felt apart from humanity, as full of friction and self-pity as a fractious misfit feeding on his miseries. Koh filled my jar again as the stingray was flayed, and as our food was cooked Eduardo sat by me in four or five minutes of silence before hesitantly saying in Spanish, "We are afraid of you."

"Why?"

"Bad things happen," he said. "We fear for our children." Eduardo's secret name in Mayan was *Nicuachinel,* he who sees into the middle of things.

Elegant Spanish escaped me. I offered him something like, "Well, that's just stupid."

But Eduardo simply said, "You go home now, please."

So I gathered my few things, got into my Volkswagen, and headed back to Resurrección. Was I thinking about how my mother died? I have no idea, but it would have been fitting. I was twenty-four then, and full of anger and psychology. I hated my art studio courses in England, but I hated going back home for the holidays, too. I felt like a boy again, an underachiever. I challenged the plastic tree my mother put up, the chilly temperature in the house, the high-cholesterol diet of my father. And I got it into my head that the family get-together needed liquor, they were far too uptight, too puritan. A furious snow was flying outside but Atticus was through arguing with me, and my mother thought she might have some groceries she could get yet, and so off we went to Antelope. A few miles west of town it got very bad, but I listened to none of my mother's cautions about the ice. My foot was flat to the floorboard even after we started to skid. "Oh honey, no!" her last words. A full hour later I woke to find myself sitting against an orange snow fence, hardly there at all, whiteness and silence filling the landscape, my neck and back aching, blood trickling from my forehead, and a sheriff's car and fire truck and ambulance were there on the highway like forgotten kid's toys. Watched four men hunch inside a milkwhite Thunderbird whose front end was crushed against a Dutch elm tree, their wide gray parkas and hurried wrestling mercifully hiding her head from me. I got up when I saw my father's truck hurrying toward the accident, and I flung myself inside the sheriff's car, anything but face him, I even hiked my coat up over my head like those guys on the hustle into jail when the photographers are feeding. But Atticus found me, of course, and I could hear the fierce control in his voice as he asked, "You okay, son?" The *him* in him could be fully silenced, if need be, he could put away his emotions like things he'd never had much use for. If fathering was his job, then he'd do it, and how he felt about his son after his wife was killed wasn't a feeling he'd entertain. We weren't ever the same after that. My shame got in the way.

Say I was thinking about that, then. And Carmen Martínez was walking down the highway in a navy blue scarf and the kind of white dress that flirts with the air, holding a huge live iguana by the tail in her right hand, possibly hunched to look at the faint pedal of its claws, how its jaws were wide and its head was lifted so it could focus on the jungle walking past. And what was she thinking of? Romance, food, homework, plans? Was she lost in childhood memories? Was she full of possibilities or was she empty, like I was then, flatlining it, a friend to my habits and nothing else, my hands hard on the wheel and my foot to the floorboard, the motor whining and stuttering, seeing nothing but a hallway of headlight ahead, no girl with an iguana too fixed on one grand idea to hear the Volkswagen behind her and get off the highway?

She never knew what hit her. I hear Carmen constantly, I'm host to the orchestra of that scream, there's no way to get it right on the page, that wail so full of hurt and outrage and not yet aware that she would be killed. And impossible, too, to say how frail and horrible and stomach-turning was the soft animal *whump* of hitting her, one blunt syllable that jolted the car and was hidden beneath the shriek of the hood's sudden misshaping as she was hoisted up into the air and her elbow or her skull, I try not to know, socked against the windshield and a fishnet of shattered glass flew in front of me even as I for the first time saw Carmen falling off into the night beside me and then behind me — just enough time for me to think *Whatwasthat?* before she was gone.

I knew, however, what *that* was; there was no mistaking that she was now in a very bad way. I shot a glance up into the rearview mirror and saw Carmen faintly heaped on the highway and then shaded in darkness. Six seconds had passed, no more, perhaps less, I could fractionate everything, still do, there are four in the mornings when I get down to cell level in the hard blast of the skirt against her flesh as the hood finds her thigh.

I hesitated just long enough to imagine a future in which I kept going, pretended nothing ugly had taken place, the fender and hood were like that, the windshield's ruin caused by a stone, a pigeon, a flaw in the glass, *Craziest dang thing happened to me last night.* But then I hit the brakes and hunted reverse and zigged and zagged a hundred yards until I found Carmen in my taillights. I have no idea how long I waited inside the car, vexed by the injustice of things, wishing she'd get up, urging her to. And then seeing that huge iguana holding on to the highway, feebly thinking, its jaws open in a kind of smile, *Wow, golly, thanx buddy.* I got a flashlight from underneath the front seat, the flashlight I'd lose in the jungle, and followed its yellow circle as it skated the highway to Carmen's body. No blood there, God what a blessing, no blood even by her head, just the blue scarf hiding half her face and the girl's beautiful arms and legs flung into ragdoll contortions. Heat was still fierce in the pavement and there was an irrational instant when I was astonished that she could stay there like that without scorching her skin. But then I felt the chill in her hand as I lifted it and laid it in front of her. The hurtle of the accident hiked up her skirt over her white cotton panties. I pulled the skirt down, then folded her legs together as I fitted my left arm underneath them and my right arm just under her neck and hauled her with great difficulty and carefulness to the high weeds at the side of the road where I laid her down. The scarf fell away then, and I saw the pretty face of a girl of seventeen who was most definitely dead, but whose black eyes were fixed on mine with the shock and fear you see in a person when what they hoped for and banked on and cannot do without wholly disappears. No accusation, no self-pity, only that look of wreckage and disappointment.

And that cooked it. I held my hands to my ears as if she were screaming still, and walked around and around in circles, just like a nut. Whether one minute or five passed, I have no idea, I was lost and foolish and whining *oh no oh no,* if the *policía* had passed by then I would have said, "Okay, take me." I was ready to go to jail, do hard time, to have one of my hands hacked off. Whether it was guilt or fright or the too-much-ness of killing the girl, I was just addled, without sand or sense, holes in my head you could fit a shoe in.

Reinhardt found me like that; tooling by in the kind of Jeep that kids rented at the hotels for a lark. Who knows what sort of Kurtz number he was pulling out there in the jungle? I was freaked enough that it hardly seemed coincidental, *of course he'd be there,* I was thinking, I probably would not have been surprised if he'd lowered on ropes from the heavens, the deus ex machina of my own doom. I heard the Jeep and shaded my eyes from the headlight glare, half-ready to hot-foot it into the flora or heave myself beneath the tires even as the Jeep halted beside me.

"I haff been looking for you," the guy said.

And then I saw that it was Reinhardt Schmidt and that he'd found the girl behind me. His foot half lifted from the Jeep's brake, *I'll just be going, forgive me;* but then he got another insight into the situation, grasped the unholy shape I was in, and hatched fragmentary plans that had for their basis that I was up to my neck in it and that it might be fortunate for him if I felt I owed him one. We probably spoke further but I have no memory of speech; I only have a picture in my mind of him knowingly stooped over Carmen, feeling for a pulse first at her wrist, then her throat, and holding the flashlight to her irises until he finally shut her lids with the first and last fingers of his hand, the horns of Satan sign. Reinhardt sat back on his haunches and looked at me with hostility before saying, "I'll take care of it."

I flush with shame when I say that I let him. Embarrassed gratitude filled me, and if I protested or tried to uphold my insipid claims to manliness, I have no recollection of it, only recall getting into his Jeep — a fatherly look as he handed me the key — and heading home like a kid with a fresh learner's permit, hardly noticing his camera flash, just rolling forward at fifteen or twenty miles per hour, far enough under the limit that even as I got near town an old woman was able to hold her gaze on my face as she hunched along the highway. *We are afraid of you.*

I hid Reinhardt's Jeep under a tarpaulin and went inside the house, filling a whiskey glass and then hunting the smell of reefer that was focused upstairs in my room. Emptied bottles of Corona were beside the headboard, a film called *Predator* was still in the VCR, and on the desk my sketch pad was opened to a page on which Reinhardt had listed, like a houseguest from hell, fourteen long-distance telephone calls he'd made to Europe and Hawaii. And that was the first time I felt the full impact of Reinhardt's taking care of it, and took to my bed in a fearsome swoon of illness, paranoia, and depression, pretty much unable to get up for two days, but sleeping no more than an hour at a time, the howling tempest inside my head demanding me fully awake at the helm. I heard Reinhardt saying over and over again, "I'll take care of it," but there were hours, too, of hearing Carmen's frustrated scream and feeling her sweet presence completely. I heard María frittering about downstairs, or talking on the phone to callers, saying I wasn't feeling well; she brought up meals I hardly touched and confessed that my friend with the blond hair kept coming by while I was away, he was so persistent, and that she'd finally let him do his laundry there. Was that all right?

You see where this is heading. Reinhardt Schmidt parked my Volkswagen beside his Jeep three days after the accident, and I heard him talking to María at the front door, offering her wildflowers for the fiesta. I got up and hurriedly put on a shirt and pants as Reinhardt headed upstairs, and he found me sitting down at my desk, rolling paper into my typewriter.

"Está bien," he said, and smiled.

"What's *bien?*"

"Todo," he said. Everything. "Look out the window."

What I saw was a faultless windshield and the fresh paint of a hood and fender repair. "Looks great, doesn't it," he said. "I went all the way to

225

Mérida for the work. I have the garage receipt, of course, and shots of the Volkswagen, too."

A flare seemed to have gone off inside my head. White hot daze and zero data, tabula rasa; I was as faceless and silent as a fallen tree.

"You haven't asked about the girl," Reinhardt said.

"You took care of her?"

"Unfortunately no. I heard a truck. Quite a situation! I got into the car and hided out in the jungle. And when I got back onto the highway again, fifteen minutes later, no more, she was gone. Spirited away." Reinhardt walked out to the hallway and hollered, *"¡María! ¡Dos Coronas por favor!"*

She hesitated but said, *"Sí, señor."*

"She was Carmen Martínez," Reinhardt said. "Sixteen years old. Eighth child in the family. Engaged to be married in June to a guy named Renaldo. She wasn't mentioned in the English newspaper, but there were two paragraphs about her in Monday's *diario*. She was buried just today."

"You're here for money."

Reinhardt sat at the foot of the mattress and happily patted a spot beside himself. I folded my arms like a hard guy and sagged against the window sash.

"You know what I told you about myself? A lot of that wasn't true."

"Boy," I said. "You think you know a guy . . ."

"I have cancer." Reinhardt icily stared at me, as if he were not communicating the full hideousness of his pain. "I have tried everything to cure it," he said, "and now I am trying some medicines you can only get in Mexico. Are they working? I hope so; probably not. But in the meantime I am losing weight and I have no money and no friends. I have a few credit cards I have stolen, but I am afraid to use them. I have a horrible room in a hotel full of Europeans on El Camino Real. I hock sunglasses on the street and I heat canned soups for dinner. It's pathetic. In the United States they have a foundation for children, I forget its name, but it fulfills the dying child's wish: to go to Disneyland, to hang out in the locker room after a Yankees game? I have wishes, too."

María halted at the doorway in torment and reluctance, with a Coca-Cola tray that supported two Coronas and two highball glasses. *"Gracias, María,"* Reinhardt said, and fastened his interested stare on her as he took the tray. She went out and his blue eyes stayed on her as if enjoying a feast. "Are you fucking her, Scott?"

Atticus used to say of such a question that he wouldn't dignify it with an answer. I filled a highball glass with beer.

Reinhardt smirked. "You *are* an innocent."

"You were talking about your last fling."

"Oh yes. A first-class flight to Frankfurt on Lufthansa, fine clothes and fabulous dinners, sex with beautiful prostitutes in the afternoons."

"You'll make each day your masterpiece."

"What a fine way of putting it!" Reinhardt sipped some beer and pressed on. "I have a fantasy that I'll finally end up in Monaco, gambling at chemin de fer just as James Bond did. If I win, I will throw the franc notes up in the air and laugh like a fat sultan as people fall to the floor for them. And if I lose, I'll say, 'I am finished!' and blow my brains out with a tiny pistol."

"A guy'd have to spend four or five hundred dollars for all that, wouldn't he?"

"Yesterday I deposited five hundred pesos in your bank account and asked for a balance. You have twenty-four thousand dollars here. You can afford to give me half that, I think."

"We're in cahoots, huh?"

"Cahoots?"

I faced the wall and faked writing 24,000, and I was just about to divide it by 2 when Reinhardt said with irritation, "Twelve thousand dollars."

"Shall we go down to the bank right now?"

Reinhardt tried to hold his smile, but it fell into a sneer. "It's six-fifteen."

Eagerness imbued my face. "Well, first thing tomorrow then?"

"I presume you know there's a fiesta Wednesday."

"Damn. And they wonder why their economy's failing."

"You can play the joke with me, of course," Reinhardt said, "but the police will not find your situation too funny. A hit-and-run accident is murder here. You'll be in jail for a very long time."

I lifted the highball glass and drank half the beer in it. Reinhardt lifted his glass, too, but felt foolish imitating me and put it back on the tray. "Do not delude yourself into thinking you are a dangerous person because you happened to kill a pretty girl. You do not have the hate, my friend. You are fatally inhibited." In proof of that, Reinhardt got up from the bed and walked out of the house. Without inhibition.

Oh honey, no.

That night I got the Monday *diario* from the gift shop in the Cortez Hotel and flipped to the obituaries while having a Gentleman Jack whiskey in the saloon. Carmen Martínez was paragraphed there just as Reinhardt said, but I wasn't up to a translation, the Spanish kept drifting sideways the harder I stared at it. So I folded the newspaper and had my whiskey glass filled again. An honorable guilt was flooding me, but with it came a hungry interest in self-preservation, and after an hour of pathos and regret I found myself trying to feature Reinhardt fulfilling his threat. I fancied a police sergeant tearing open an envelope and finding a white page filled with paste-on letters snipped from magazines — English about the hit-and-run driver who killed Carmen Martínez. And there, too, would be the flash camera shots of the girl and my Volkswagen's rear license plate, and behind them the body shop receipts from Mérida. And then, perhaps, Stuart would be at my house in his American consul suit. "Would it be possible to *chat* with you for a bit?"

Even in my malaise and my shipwreck of rationality, I was not hard pressed to come up with a simple alibi. Reinhardt visited me at my *casita* where I'd stayed for a few days, hard at work, and seeing me wrestling to fit a too-large canvas into my Volkswagen, offered to swap cars with me. I took him up on it and he must have hit Carmen while I parked his Jeep in my driveway. Wasn't he trying to hide his accident from me when he got the car fixed in Mérida? I fell low with the flu and forgot that we hadn't changed cars again. María could vouch for the fact that I was home for two full days, and that Reinhardt brought the Volkswagen back Tuesday night. Yes, I noticed the fresh paint and new windshield. Reinhardt told me he'd hit a wild deer and got the car repaired for me in Mérida.

I hated the shameless face I'd wear for the *jefe,* so full of innocence and fraudulent worry about my hindrance to justice. And yet it did not seem to me that a great wrong would have been righted if I were jailed. I figured Renata ought to know about Reinhardt, though, just in case his frustration found her, but when I telephoned her it was Stuart, of course, who answered and asked, "Whom shall I say is calling?" I heard Stuart's hand cover the mouthpiece for half a minute, but it finally lifted enough for me to hear Stuart say, "You can't, you *can not!*" And then the hand held on more securely until Renata blithely said, *"¡Hola!"*

"Is this a bad time to talk?"

"You must be psychic."

"Are you going to the play reading tomorrow night?"

"I'm in the cast, Scott."

"Oh, that's right. Well then, we'll talk there, okay?"

"Easy on the whiskey, fella."

"We'll talk, though?"

"You're penciled in."

"Stuart's pouting, isn't he," I said.

Renata just said, "Ta-ta," and put the phone handset in its cradle.

Late that night, just after two, I heard a great splash in my swimming pool and then the regular thrashing of Reinhardt doing laps. I felt confident the house doors were locked. I found I was able to go back to sleep.

I got up at eight Wednesday morning and tried to jog off a hangover with four miles on hard sand that still held the sheen of seawater. Kids were lighting firecrackers inside the huge girdered rooms of the four-story hotel that was just going up, and families were hauling sheets of plywood from the site to put their folding chairs on or to hoist up for fiesta shade.

María had the day off, so I cooked *huevos rancheros* for myself, skimmed some articles in *Art Journal* by the pool, got into blue jeans and a white shirt, and headed out to the *casita* on my Harley-Davidson at noon, halting on the highway to peer worriedly at the place where Señorita Carmen Martínez was killed.

Weeks had passed since I last painted in my studio, but there were fresh tire tracks on the forest path heading in to the house. I failed to be surprised. The hinge of the front door hasp had been pried from the jamb with my garden spade, and the shackled padlock hung there uselessly. Wrecked as my studio was inside, the harm seemed more petulant and hot-tempered than intimidating. My Radiola boom box was there along with my tapes, so sheer theft wasn't the point. Jars of turpentine had been spilled and free paints had been flung on my unfinished canvases in a kind of high school violence that seemed in faint homage to Hans Hofmann's art. Chairs were tipped, of course, a drafting table was overturned, torn pages from my sketch books skittered on the floor like fall leaves as I walked about assessing the havoc. Even the pathos of the fury — shirts pulled from their hangers, faucet water left running, a paring knife stabbed into my self-portrait — ought to have informed me it was not Reinhardt who did it, far more like him to clean me out — *Wow, thanks for the pictures!* — but I was too focused on him as my antagonist to make fine discriminations. Hours frittered by as I tidied the place and fastened the hasp to the jamb with new screws, and I was so zeroed in on my housekeeping chores that it was only when I was halfway down the hill again that I felt an ooze of suspicion and hurried back inside the *casita* to find out if the beautiful walnut gun case that Frank gave me at Christmas was still hidden in the closet. Well, the gun case was there; the Winchester shotgun and a handful of green Federal shells were gone.

Which was why, when evening came, I was a silent, hand-wringing, brooding lost soul, full of subtext and umbrage and haunted glances, contributing nothing to Renata's and Stuart's thinking chatter at The Scorpion until Renata picked up on my dispiritedness and I confessed that my studio had been broken into, no big deal really, but what a pain, blah blah blah.

"Was anything stolen?" Renata asked, and I hung there over a gin and tonic, wondering how she'd take the news that the shotgun was gone, figuring she could only be frightened by that, and finally saying, no, nothing had been stolen, thank God. Wished they'd taken the horrible painting I was working on.

Stuart paid for the drinks because I found I'd mislaid my American Express card somewhere. Stuart simpered. "Have you checked all the bars?"

"Good idea. I'll have to do that."

Renata talked about the ferocity in Tennessee Williams's plays on our stroll to the Marriott Hotel, and then I trailed away from Stuart and her, cattling my way with a hundred others to the trough of the fancy fiesta table, finagling a frosted pitcher of margarita from a waiter and becoming fundamental with it, like some high school lout who'd crashed the party, while Renata and various others read parts in *The Night of the Iguana.* I fully intended to talk to Renata about Reinhardt Schmidt and Carmen Martínez and the hazards and misfortunes of my life, but I had fallen into the alcoholic's habit of first things first, of needing the heat and flush of hard liquor to feel myself, of finding forthrightness and confidence only after a heavy fix. But the old *kaboom* never came even after a full pitcher, and when Renata was finally free after the play, she was in no mood for me. She was up front beside the podium under the frothy watch of Stuart and in a flock of friends who congratulated her for the intricate shadings she'd brought to Ava Gardner's role. And there I was, the horse's ass, four sheets to the wind, hazy-eyed and hearty, my walk a confusion of tilts and pitches, saying "Great stuff!" so loudly it was like a whiskey glass smashed to the floor. Unforgiveness shot at me from fourteen faces, but Renata forced a smile and said, "You flatter me."

Stuart shouted, *"Don't* humor him, Renata! Aren't you *insulted?* He's drunk as a *lord!"*

" 'How like a man, is Man, who rises late and gazes on his unwashed dinner plate and gazes on the bottles, empty too, all gulphed in last night's loud long how-do-you-do, — although one glass yet holds a gruesome bait — how like to Man is this man and his fate, still drunk and stumbling through the rusty trees to breakfast on stale rum, sardines, and peas.' " In the silence of hostility I said, "End of poem. 'Eye-opener,' by Malcolm Lowry. Englishman, like you, Lowry was. Kin at all?"

"You silly knave," Stuart sighed.

Renata just turned away.

Offended and foolish, I offered all a fraternal smile — *See how harmless I am?* — and hauled myself from that fiesta in the childhood of drunkenness, full of fury and incoherence, falling to my hands and knees more than once, hearing the boom and pop and whistle of fireworks from the Zuma Hotel farther north, seeking, God help me, a friendlier place where people drank like I did, faintly remembering a hellish cantina that was called La Cucaracha and ought to have been on Avenida de las Pulgas but was not, and finally hitting upon, in a kind of trance, my house on Avenida del Mar.

And there against the high white wall, as forgotten as a trike, was my Winchester shotgun. I felt heat in its nickel barrel as I hefted it, and I teetered off balance as I broke it open. A green shell flew out that I failed to follow in flight, and I hunted it for three or four minutes before giving up. I sniffed the shell chamber like a hound and affirmed the shotgun had been fired, and I shouted to the night, "Reinhardt! You forgot your persuader!" I was thinking that was terrifically funny, high comedy, the guy's got a zinger for every occasion, as I opened the front door with my key, failing to notice that the key pulled no bolt from its home. I heard the hush and scratch and ping of clothes tumbling in the kitchen dryer, and I heard Sinatra singing "Where or When" as I hulked my way to the dining room with the shotgun hanging over my forearm. And Reinhardt Schmidt was there on the Indian floor rug, flat out on his back and his face in red horror, the flesh raked off its architecture by that twelve-gauge shotgun shell.

I fell to my knees in the hallway, frail as an old

man, letting the shotgun ease off my forearm and clank onto the pink marble floor. What is the opposite of worship? I have never felt so alone and hexed and loathsome and unblessed as when I watched Reinhardt's blood ooze from him, wondering in my drunkenness if there were doctor things I ought to do, and then reading the dining room mirror where *"Asesino,"* murderer, was printed in Renata's lipstick.

Worry and fear got me half sober again, for I was positive then that Reinhardt's killer thought Reinhardt was me, he was a friend or relative of Carmen Martínez and he'd be back again for vengeance when he found out about his mistake. Even in the free fall of far too much juice I got on my feet and walked through to the kitchen and gave a try at a chronology, though Reinhardt's murderer was a fill-in-the-blank to me then, not Renaldo Cruz, finding the full glass door to the pool that I'd locked was jimmied open, Reinhardt's green plastic laundry basket was on the kitchen countertop with a box of Cheer inside it, his whiskey glass was on the floor by the stereo, and Reinhardt's left hand was beside it in a kind of offering while the half of his face that gunshot hadn't ravaged was as indifferent as a waiter's.

Even as I write this I have no idea how Renaldo Cruz found out that I killed his *novia.* But the forest is full of eyes along that highway, he may have been informed about a crazy *rubio* who'd

237

flashed by just before Carmen was hit, and then found my house in the forest and ransacked it and stole my fancy shotgun. Even children in the fields could have told him where I oh so flagrantly lived in town. Was he tracking me from then on? Or was he tracking Reinhardt by mistake? Was it just the fiesta that forced Renaldo to wait until Wednesday night to hike himself up over the pool's high fence and jimmy the full glass door? And then did he walk through the upstairs rooms, handling my possessions, hating the differences he saw between my life in Mexico and the harder one of his family and friends? But he wrecked nothing then, took nothing but Renata's brass lipstick case, possibly thinking of it as a present for his sister. Renaldo must have hidden inside, focusing on his purpose, until he heard the front door open. Even then he must have held himself in check as Reinhardt hauled his laundry inside the house and filled the dryer with my clothes, filled the washer with his. Was Renaldo in the hallway while Reinhardt filled his glass with whiskey? Was Reinhardt carrying his whiskey from the kitchen to the dining room when Renaldo lifted the shotgun? Was there a moment when Renaldo saw him and hesitated? Did Reinhardt look up in surprise? Were things said? Was Reinhardt inserting the Sinatra CD when he heard footsteps and turned? Was he kneeling by the stereo when he put his whiskey glass down on the floor? And did he hear the shotgun as the hammer was cocked? Was he shocked at the sound? Did he think that Renaldo was me? And did Reinhardt smirk when he turned from the stereo? Was there time for Reinhardt to say in English that he was not who Renaldo thought he was? How long before Renaldo found out he was wrong?

Well, it was too much for me then, far more than I could handle in that condition with my head sending out flashes and flares. Even things as simple as the alphabet were slewing off into "e, f, green, hello." *I'll have to think about this later,* I thought, and knew I'd have a host of years of thinking of nothing else.

Shall I confess my envy for Reinhardt then? Suddenly he seemed full of such certainty and purpose. And it was I whose life seemed in chaos, whose innermost fears and longings and beliefs were a mystery to himself. We were at the crisis point in our plot. We were at the spot where our hero is forced to make a choice. You are in trouble, I finally thought to myself. You'd better do something quick.

Looked at my watch. A quarter to eleven. I got up and carried the dining chairs into the kitchen. Skidded the dining table off the Indian rug and against the full glass doors. I got down on my knees beside Reinhardt and gingerly lifted him until he was lying across my knees, as conquered as Christ in a pietà. I felt as hollow as a child, felt how unfair and cruel and unjust it was that our likenesses had killed him for me and there was no unkilling him, no way of undoing the deed or defending myself but to hide it.

So I heaved the huge load of Reinhardt up onto my left thigh and hitched my back until I found a way to get up to my feet and haul him to the hallway, his head knocking dully against the wall once, his huaraches hitting together as I laid him by the front door. I folded in half a dining room rug that was heavy with blood and then halved it again and slung it behind me as I tilted into the hallway with it. I found white vinegar and a sponge under the kitchen sink, washed *Asesino* from the dining room mirror, and hunted the floor and walls for blood, fastidious to a fault, then looked along the hallway for telltales of our lurch and wobble to the door. I thoroughly rinsed out the sponge and hand-washed the sink, then carried the dining chairs out from the kitchen, skidded the table back, and tidied the room.

I fortified myself with whiskey from Reinhardt's glass and frowned at myself in the Cinemascope of the dining room mirror. My face was white, the life flushed from it. My eyes were scary, yelling *Don't cross me.* Even I shied from them. I found inkblots of blood on the front of my white oxford shirt and I got it half off when I freaked at the sudden noise of the telephone, fierce as a bayonet that ringing. My hand went for it, hesitated, and finally let it ring, four times, five. Was it Renata or someone else? *(Well, you see I'm kind of busy now. I have to hide a guy's body.)* Wrestling out of the shirt, I took it out the kitchen door to the green garbage container, pushing it beneath the trash already there, then got into a hot, gray Stanford T-shirt that was falling with my clothes in the dryer. Emptying the full load into his green plastic basket and pitching Reinhardt's wet clothes into the dryer, I found his handwriting on a notepad that hung next to the kitchen phone, a Mexico City number that I found the presence of mind to dial.

A female voice told me in Spanish that it was the American Express Travel Office. I got out my wallet and flipped it open as I asked if she spoke English.

"Yes, sir."

My Colorado driver's license was missing, too. I got the picture. "Uh, I just put in a reservation for a flight but I think I may have screwed up and given you the numbers from my corporate card."

"Your name, sir?"

"Cody, last name; first name, Scott."

"Momentito." I heard her tapping and scrolling. I was frenetic and hair-rakingly jazzed, functioning at the high speed of cocaine and kicking the kitchen drawers with my knee until she fi-

nally said, "Lufthansa to Frankfurt?"

"*Sí.*"

She read the numbers.

"Oh, good," I said. "*Perfecto.* And where can I find the tickets again?"

"Same place," she said. "Our office in Resurrección."

"*Muchas gracias, señora.*"

"*De nada.*"

I hung up the telephone and flicked off the house lights as I hurried out to the hallway and took a full breath or two before I found the courage to get down there beside him and force my hand inside his trouser pockets. I found his wallet, but my American Express card and Colorado license weren't in it. I felt like hitting him in the head. I hunted inside his front trouser pockets. Empty. I fumed for half a minute, sitting back on my heels, and then heard Reinhardt telling me about his horrible hotel room on El Camino Real, full of Europeans, he'd said, and I presumed it was a *posada* called El Marinero, the sailor. I left him in the hallway and locked the front door and got into the Volkswagen. I tuned the car radio to a Texas station that found its way to Resurrección late at night, hearing fools on a talk show as I drove to Boystown and searched El Camino Real for El Marinero.

The night manager was hulking over the high front desk, his elbows holding down the bloodily illustrated pages of a wrestling magazine. "I have forgotten my key," I said, and he looked up with a frown that was halfway between boredom and suspicion.

"Your name?"

"Reinhardt Schmidt."

He held his gaze on me for a long time, as if he were trying to grow an idea, *Say, something fishy's going on here,* but then he sighed and got the key for number 13 from its pigeonhole and went back to his magazine as I gingerly ascended the staircase, my hand faintly squeaking along the handrail, as cool, I figured, as Ray Milland in *Dial M for Murder*. We were not completely in touch with our feelings.

And then I was inside Reinhardt's room. I felt doomed by the hoard he'd filled it with in the weeks of his hopeless cure. Wonder bread and Coca-Cola and Oreo cookies, a hot plate and a case of Campbell's soup, a high tower of foreign crime paperbacks, a box full of sunglasses with price tags on them, his floor littered with photos and contact sheets and Kodak film cartons. I was too harried for time to do more than haul out his green suitcase and fill it with a good portion of his clothes and fancier things. His film and proofs I heaped in a box that had been shipped there from Holland, and I stowed the box in the hallway to get later. In the bathroom I found a plastic sack from the *farmacia,* and I filled it with all the elixirs and pills that tumbled from behind the mirror of the medicine cabinet.

Would the hotel call in the police if Reinhardt was missing? I phoned the front desk and told the night manager in English that I was Reinhardt Schmidt and that I'd be sightseeing further inland for a while but wanted to keep the room. I heard him rummage around and get the hotel bill. "Of course, Mr. Smeet," he said. "And do you still want to pays on your Visa cart?"

"Sí, gracias."

Without feeling, he said, "Thanks is for you."

Then I was out of there, flipping the door handle sign so no maid would disturb the place and skidding the Holland box and Reinhardt's full suitcase down the hallway. At first I thought I'd toss it all in the barrio, *Your prayers have been answered,* freebies from heaven, but I was afraid I'd be seen by the up-all-nights there, and so I heaved the suitcase and box inside the car and headed back to the house.

And I got frightened because the front door wouldn't force open more than an inch at first. I felt Reinhardt was there and fully alive and fighting me for the keep of the house, but I firmed my effort until I was inside and found his body had rolled against the front door in some zombie move, his face looking up at me from the hallway floor in a fractured way, half of it as red and tortured as a scream, half as familiar and at peace

244

as a head on a sofa pillow.

I hurried up to my room, hung Reinhardt's clothes among my own, and tucked his green suitcase away in the closet of the guest bedroom. I forgot to hunt my passport and visa. I took Reinhardt's medicines and the *farmacia* sack downstairs, tossed his medicines into the green garbage container, then put his whiskey glass and the full green Jameson's bottle in the sack. I frankly thought I was cooking, no flies on me, my footprints wiped away by the tide.

I finally ransacked the box that was full of his photos and contact sheets, finding pictures of myself running in gym shorts, filling Renata's wineglass with a *vino tinto,* holding a match to a cigar on the terrace, getting into my Volkswagen outside Printers Inc — fifty shots, maybe more; Reinhardt watching me from afar, waiting for his chance, and getting it, as he knew he would. I failed to find the photographs of the Volkswagen on the highway, the fender and windshield damage, whatever it was that he'd hoped to use against me, but I presumed they were in his stash somewhere and I hauled it outside and far down the hill to the Maya, where I heaved the full box into a green Dumpster behind the hotel's kitchen.

Then I ran back up to the house, where I hoisted a folded and off-putting rug and flicked off the lights in the house and got Reinhardt into the Volkswagen somehow. Such waltzing is not easy. I have no memory of it really, only of walking away from the half-opened passenger door and the yellow glow of the dome light just above the hideousness of his face and finding his sitting there satisfactory, a fine composition, just a guy waiting in the night. I walked back to turn up the Volkswagen's radio, heard the first minute of news, and jolted shut the door. And then I finicked around the first floor of the house again, found the shotgun in the hallway, hit the lights, and walked out.

I headed out to the jungle, my hands holding hard on to the wheel, fearing that if I lifted them I'd fly away with the jim-jams, half my head in some funky horror movie with the formerly dead just biding his time to have his terrible revenge, the half I'll simply call less insane feeling sympathy for Reinhardt and trying to gain some points in Heaven by insisting that it was a work of mercy to honorably bury the dead. I was harnessed to that: Hide the guy in the rug, heave him into a pit, tamp down the fertile earth with a garden spade. *Reinhardt Schmidt, you say? Oh, he disappeared long ago.*

I parked at the foot of the hill, got the shotgun, and killed the engine but kept the Volkswagen's headlights on so I could find the path. Whine of insects. Ticking engine. And no other sounds but those of undulant waves softly achieving the shore. I flicked on the ceiling lights in the studio and sought to put on some music, failing to notice that I hit the REC button on my Radiola tape player, failing, too, to notice the silence of its furtive recording as I fell into habits that now seem absurd: limbering brushes in a turpentine jar, hanging an unfinished canvas on the easel, squeezing out a few paints on my hand palette, heating water for coffee. I have no memory of fitting the filter into the funnel, but I did it, measuring out the hazelnut and watching with nary a flinch, non compos mentis, until the water finally tumbled into a boil. I filled the funnel and finally went for him.

Eduardo's kids were there at the foot of the hill, walking through the headlight beams and getting up on the Volkswagen's running board to peer at Reinhardt. His face was turned away from them so that he must have seemed unhurt, just resting, and the blackness, the familiar car, his blond hair, and our faint resemblance were enough that I heard a teenaged girl named Elba say in a hushed voice, *"Cotziba,"* Lord Artist, and then the kids got down to the ground again and Elba silenced them as they hurried away.

That was when it hit me: just trade places, let Reinhardt be me, be my sundog. I'd find a new life and kill off my failures, my history of ruin, the high hum that played behind my blood tango with chance and mystery. It seemed so easy and necessary. I haven't felt so free since I was four.

I put the key in the ignition of my Harley-Davidson, as if I'd gone out there on it, and I opened the door on the Volkswagen's passenger's side and pulled Reinhardt to me, holding him in a hard embrace as I fought my way up the hill to the charnel house. Where I arranged Reinhardt in the torn green wingback chair and snugged his right thumb inside the shotgun's trigger guard before angling its stock to the floor and letting it fall aside. My little science project. Then I took the shotgun outside and fired it at the moon. The hugeness of that noise got to me until I heard, hard on its heels, the rat-a-tat of firecrackers in the jungle and I figured I'd simply become another merrymaker in the fiesta. I handkerchiefed the trigger housing with turpentine just in case the Mexican police tried to lift fingerprints from it — hardly likely — and then I held Reinhardt's hands to it, gumming up the metal, and arranged the shotgun on the floor. But his blood was trickling a fresh path along his throat, and I ascertained that his bloodstains were all wrong, hardening underneath his upper arm and back, finding the shank and welt of his Cole-Haan shoe. I fought his clothes and shoes off him and, as calm and confident as an undertaker, fitted him into blue jeans and a hot yellow shirt that were hanging in the closet. The Radiola got to the final inch of its winding tape and clunked off, but I was clueless about what that meant.

Walked out to the high cliffs over the sea and flung his shoes out into the night; Reinhardt's clothes I hurriedly wadded up for burial in the forest. I tilted his head to the left as if it were jolted that way by the force of the shotgun blast and finished the mise-en-scène by putting my Swiss wristwatch on him and filching the pesos from both our wallets and tucking mine in his blue jeans. And for the first time I felt a twinge of guilt over the damage I'd be doing to my father and Renata. But I was too far down the road to do more than snatch a sheet of paper from my sketch pad and write on it with a felt-tip pen, "No one is to blame." Hardly enough, I knew, not one of those things your father would read and think, *Wow, what a relief!*, but I signed the note anyway and I finally left the front door open and the coffee heating on the hot plate as I skidded and fell down the hill, frankly hoping that the house would burn down or creatures would make havoc of Reinhardt, frustrating identification.

I have lost all sympathy, I know. Cold, fearful, reckless, full of self-pity, I was so free of taking responsibility for my actions that I seem hardly even there. If I was not, in fact, a murderer, it was because that term did not fully cover the awfulness of all that I'd done. Even then I knew I was not going to get away with it, but I was too far into the killed-himself bit to not try to finish it. I hauled the bloodstained rug and Reinhardt's clothes far into the forest, my flashlight flaring over the tails of hurrying things that I tried not to think about, and I finished the worst of my harrowing ordeal by burying the evidence with a garden spade that I then put in the car. I headed into Resurrección in the Volkswagen, not thinking of the hurt of a funeral for family and friends, only thinking of Scott and how he could flee the country and find a new life. I fell into the old patterns of childhood, holding it all in, confessing nothing to my father, hoping to bide my time in hiding like I used to in my upstairs room. *Maybe he won't notice.* Well, it was madness, I admit it, but rationality offered no upside return, it would give me nothing but grief. Even telling Renata was impossible. If she helped me in any way she'd be an accessory after the fact. She could be imprisoned even if I wasn't. And Renata was my only hope of finally pulling off the scam. So I halted in front of the public telephone near the *jardín* and dialed Renata's number. An office light was on in Printers Inc. Stuart at his bookkeeping. A few policemen were laughing and smoking cigarettes in front of the *comisaría de policía*. I held my breath until Renata picked up.

"Hi," I said. "Is it too late to talk?"

"It's one-fifteen. Are you able?"

"Sobered up," I told her. Agitation and fright got me turning with the phone until I was staring across the gardens at the huge pink parish church.

In its foundation was a former window that plywood was nailed over, but the plywood seemed framed with a filament of light, as if a forty-watt bulb were burning in the cellar. "I hear voices behind you," I said.

"The cast. We're still having a little party here."

"Oh." My purpose, I remembered, was to tie up loose ends. "Look: I forgot where I left my car."

"Again?" She seemed happy and tipsy and prepared to find a lot to laugh about.

"I figure it must be near the *jardín.* You've still got a key for it, don't you?"

"Yes."

"I have something to finish in the jungle. I'm going out there on the hog. Will you try to find my car and take it back to the house?"

She held the phone so that the female voices behind her went away. She may have walked to another room. "Are you all right?" she asked. "You sound so strange."

"Really tired, is all. Really really tired."

"You're waiting for your spirits to catch up."

I'd forgotten I'd told her that story.

She whispered temptingly, "Shall I come out?"

I practically fell under the irony. I felt like the butt of a joke. Everything seemed to have changed and she'd become a possibility that it

251

was now impossible for me to have. "Don't," I said.

My tone forced her to hesitate before she said, "It's just that you sounded like you could use a friend."

"Give me a few days. I have a lot of work to do and I don't want to be disturbed."

Even that she found funny. "I hate to break it to you, but you *are* disturbed, Scott."

And then there was nothing further to do but say, "I love you," and hang up.

I was still peering at the *parroquia.* Eduardo's term for the parish church was from the Mayan, the house of he who invents himself. Self-invention was so much what I was about that heading over there seemed to me a stroke of genius. Walking across the *jardín* in the wee-hours silence of the Old Town, I felt graced with the first clear picture of a finer life, out of harm's way, hiding out in the old church's cellar, huddling in the noontime shade with my hand held out for coins.

The front doors were locked, but a rough plank door below the great bell tower was open and I found my way inside. I touched a font and half expected a hiss from the holy water as I crossed myself. A hundred or more votive candles provided only a faint yellow light, and it was half a minute before I realized a hunched old Mexican woman was in there with me, kissing her fingertips and softly applying them to the lips of the carpenter, San José. Easing my way down the main aisle between the black pews, I faced architecture and saints and pictures that were familiar to some sane and ancient part of me. I felt aware, wonder-filled, wise, it was far better than the best trip with peyote. I quietly sidestepped through the gate of the high altar's railing, genuflected to the tabernacle, and headed into the priest's sacristy. I knew my way, knew that there was a semicircular halfway of brick that formed the perimeter of the apse, and halfway along the hallway there would be a gray door to a stairway. I walked to that gray door and gingerly went down the stairway to a hardly lighted cellar, finding the railing with my hand, ducking under the huge floor joists, getting used to the green swamp odors of earth and human sewage.

The block walls of the first mission church were still preserved along the foundation, and the furniture of a few centuries was under the great floor of the building, a fine fur of dust on the old pews and prie-dieux, gray veils of cobwebs faintly waggling in the air, and in the haven and haze and junkyard of that basement were poor Mexicans who'd found a hard kind of sanctuary there, twenty or more of them watching me with the unsurprised gaze of the frequently desperate. A gray old man with a face peppered by skin cancer was praying the rosary in a harsh whisper as he stared at me. Without judgment. And then he pointed toward a flattened cardboard box with the name Hotpoint on it. And it was as if my place had been prepared for me. I knelt down on that mat and felt I'd found my future. And my tremendous exhaustion so hammered me that I fell to my hands and knees and then fainted.

Woke up Thursday morning with the bleak people there staring at me. Talking in my sleep, I presumed, but their stares and curiosity flipped the paranoia switch and I was positive they were in on the conspiracy — friends or family of Carmen or Renaldo just waiting for the opportunity to grapple. No proportion to my fear. Enemies everywhere. I hunkered in a corner of that great dark basement, my head hurting with hangover, my eyes flicking toward every sound, until I'd freaked the Mexicans there so much that they hung out in a far part of the room and held their children back when the wolfman walked to a green bucket for water and, just to be grandly theatrical, tilted my head far into it and drank from it like a horse.

With nothing to do, I got a kid to go buy me a pen and spiral notebook, and I fussed up a page or two of forlorn prose about my plight. And then I just fretted and stewed until nightfall, holding my hands out in laths of sunlight that fell through a high window exhaust fan, watching the twitches of stress in my right thumb and first finger, lifting up my khaki pants cuffs to see my calf muscles bunch and crawl as if there were furtive rodents under the skin. Was it a head case or delirium tremens? It felt like mescaline or peyote, the kind of far-out high you get where even your thoughts seem to have a sandpaper texture. I was certain that Reinhardt had been discovered, but I still wasn't sure if the police fell for my fabrication. If they didn't, if they knew it was Reinhardt, then I would be wanted for murder and there was nothing I could do to prove that I didn't, in fact, kill him. Wasn't it my gun, in my jungle house? Didn't I have the motive and opportunity? Hadn't I tried to hide what I'd done? Were these, Your Honor, the actions of an innocent man? And if I attempted a full explanation, I'd have to mention Carmen Martínez, the hit-and-run, and I'd be just as parboiled as far as the police were concerned. And if they thought it was me out there in that green wingback chair, I was pretty sure Renaldo didn't. Even if he thought it was me on the dining room floor, he'd have heard about the blond American who shotgunned himself in the jungle and he would not have heard about my maid finding a murder in the house on Avenida del Mar, and he'd get to the truth in no time. Each heartless, intricate move I'd made Wednesday night now seemed foolish. Renaldo could murder me now and I wouldn't even be missed. You are dead, man, I thought, and both senses of that sentence applied.

A kid wandered in at six with a box of soft tacos filled with the spiced meat of iguana. My fellow inmates there failed to tell him to be afraid of me and I still looked enough like an American with money that he finally sought me out. I bought two tacos and hungrily finished one while I got out a roll of pesos and gave him thirty dollars' worth, telling the kid to find me huaraches, plastic sunglasses, a blue bandana to hide my blond hair under, and an old cowboy hat. Stuart's beggar was sitting on a pew, eating refried beans from a can, and I got him to exchange his fetid denim shirt for my fresh gray Stanford T-shirt. The kid was back inside of an hour with foul but useful things he may have found in his father's closet. I got into my off-putting costume, and skulked down the side streets like Jack the Ripper until I found a *tienda* selling the Thursday *diario* — a hard look from the grocer at the sunglassed guy on the skids. And there it was on page four, *suicidio* in the headline and a few rough facts about Scott Cody and the *triste pérdida* of the *famoso artista de los Estados Unidos*. Cipiano's mortuary, no rosary planned, and a noontime funeral Mass at the Church of the Resurrection two days hence. Which meant Atticus would probably already be on his way down.

I found darkness wherever I could as I strolled

up Avenida del Mar to number 69 and forced my way inside like Renaldo had. Even in the moonlight I could tell that María had thoroughly cleaned the house and waxed the dining room floor where the rug had been. In the night of the kitchen I got out whiskey and filled a juice glass with it, and then I went upstairs to my room and hauled out from beneath the desk the plastic wastebasket that María too often forgot to empty, sifting out of it cigar ashes and papers and the first-of-the-week *diario* with the obituary for Carmen Martínez. Went into the bathroom, tightly shut the door, and flicked on the fluorescent lights over the sink, translating the paragraph carefully this time, and finding that Carmen was survived by a father and mother and four sisters, and by a fiancé named Renaldo Cruz. I felt certain he was the one. I sliced out the obituary with a razor blade, folded the clipping in my pants pocket, stuffed the *diario* in the wastepaper basket, took a phone directory back into the bathroom, and, as I got out of my black jeans and festering shirt, looked up the name Cruz. There were fourteen of them, and I feared my Spanish wasn't good enough to handle whatever I had to say. I took a quick shower and toweled off and then wiped down the stall to hide that I'd been there. Changed into my old Mexican clothes again, flicked off the bathroom lights, then hunted my passport and visa in my handkerchief drawer. Looked at the quartz clock by the bed — five minutes to nine — then looked through the telephone directory with a penlight and dialed the American Express travel office in town just before it closed.

"Bueno," a young woman answered.

I asked the office clerk in Spanish if she was still holding a Lufthansa ticket for Scott Cody.

When did I order it?

Wednesday night.

"Momentito," she said, and then she confirmed that she did have it, but I was too late for the flight out tonight.

Was it good for any night?

Of course; it was full fare. But I'd need to make a reservation.

Would she have it delivered to 69 Avenida del Mar?

"Mañana," she said, and only after I hung up did I think that *mañan*a was a flexible term and could mean either morning or tomorrow or sometime in the future. I tried to telephone the office again, but it was then after nine.

I foolishly put the visa and passport down somewhere in the darkness when I hunted Reinhardt's suitcase in the walk-in closet of the guest bedroom. I couldn't remember if I'd got everything out of Reinhardt's luggage but felt around with my hand and knew that I had, and I shut the hard-sided suitcase tight with a red shock cord.

And forgot about the passport and visa. My own private attention deficit disorder. Then I heard a truck halt in the street right in front of the place. I held my breath and heard singing on the truck radio and the talking of four or five men. A flashlight beam glanced through the high window of the stairway, walked along the house, and then shot into the kitchen and flooded the dining room. But that was all. Half a minute passed and I heard shoes and the chunk of a truck door and the singing gradually faded as the truck rolled down the hill. I hustled down the stairs then, and out through the pool door, and trotted along the hard wet sand of high tide to the *centro*.

Printers Inc would have closed by nine, but on the off chance that Renata would still be there, I walked down the alley behind the bookstore and looked in through the window of the storage room and its green-curtained doorway. A flash of a feminine hand holding a paperback, then nothing, then a plaid skirt and the fluorescent lights fluttering off from the front of the store to the rear. I tried the door handle, dodged inside, and held myself against a high bookcase, in darkness. Renata walked into the storage room with four hardbacks that she forced into a box. I tackled her against me and whacked her mouth shut with my hand. "Don't scream," I hissed. "It's Scott."

I felt her shock at first, that hard stiffening of fear, and then she changed as she got who it was, struggling fiercely, wrestling and whimpering, falling away and kicking at me, far more wrath than worry to it, and I just held her more tightly, hoarsely whispering into her hair, "Shhh. Shhh. Stop it. Are you alone?"

She relented a little and nodded.

I let Renata go and she turned and angrily flung herself at me again, her fists hitting hard at my chest and face and head for a full minute, shrieking calumnies and dirty words, shrieking how could I do that to her? put her through that? talk to her now? it was horrible. Et cetera. I accepted it all like a proper penance, and when she grew tired I held her away from me.

"I'm sorry," I said. "I hoped to keep you out of it."

"Well you *didn't*. Creep! I had to lie to the police. And I had no *clue* about you or what the truth was. What the hell is going on? Who was he?"

"Reinhardt Schmidt. Did they buy it?"

"The police? Yes, I think so. At least, they're not investigating." She felt her mouth. "You hurt my mouth with your hand."

I held her face toward the office light and looked. "It's not bleeding."

Renata twisted away and again struck my chest, but weakly now, hardly more than a pat, an emotional metaphor. "You have no idea how I've *hated* you today!" She fumed for a moment, then threw back her tangled hair and flung closed the green hanging draperies, shielding us from the front windows. "What happened?"

"I found Reinhardt dead in the dining room Wednesday night."

"Why in your house? Who was he?"

"I have no time to go into that now."

"Make time."

Sighing at the fatigue of it, I said, "Reinhardt's just a guy I met who was trying to get money from me. Why he was killed and by whom is a mystery. Okay? Wednesday night, though, I thought it looked like I'd done it, so I tried to hide what had happened. I was drunk, and scared. I had a hard time figuring out what to do."

She hotly said, "Don't you *dare* talk to me about being scared! You know what he *looked* like when I found him? You know how that *hurts?* My first thought was that it was you. And all afternoon I *wished* it was. Stuart forced me to call your father. What fun that was." She harshly wiped both eyes with her palms. "*God,* I resent these tears!"

"What does Stuart know?"

Renata sat against the box of hardbacks and hung her head as she got out a tissue. "Nothing."

"Maintain that."

She touched her nose with the tissue and scowled. "You really are crazy, you know. Your father's flying down. Am I supposed to keep

261

playing your stupid charade?"

"You have to, I think. Don't let on to my father and he'll leave right after the funeral. I have to get out of Mexico first. We'll straighten everything out after that."

"Everyone will be relieved. Won't they. You depend on that."

"I hurt a lot of people. I know that. But it was truly self-preservation."

Renata was quiet with thought. "He was killed in your house. Are you in danger?"

"I have to lie low, that's all. Look: I forgot my passport and visa in the guest room. Will you try to find them for me tomorrow?"

"I'll have to try to get them with your father there."

"Stay the night if you have to. You can pull it off. And see if a Lufthansa ticket was delivered. María hides my mail in the dining room sideboard."

"Lufthansa."

"To Germany. Reinhardt ordered it."

"I really really hate this."

She was still sitting there when I went out.

Half a lifetime ago an international consortium of petroleum companies invited some regional oil producers to a conference in New York, and since I was painting there I threw a party in the East Village for my father. But I was too hyped, too shy of his powers of detection, and I spent the night hustling out of whichever room he entered; he even found me behind the kitchen door once. "Why are you so spooked, son?" he asked. The question was rhetorical, he only had to fleetingly meet my friends to know how I'd failed to live up to his standards. But there was no blame in him, no scold or pontification, he was never one of those not-in-my-house-you-don't fathers, there was only that calm, see-all, X-ray stare that told me *This is not healthy and you know it.*

Waking up in the church basement on Friday, I got the usual frightened watchfulness, the mothers hushing their children's questions, but also Stuart's beggar, Hector, tilted over me on his crutches and informed me that four Mexican men had walked through the basement the night before, wondering aloud where the blond American was. "We didn't know," he told me in Spanish, implying that no one there felt especially protective of me. And then he gave me my father's stare before going off on his rounds.

I took the hint and from nine until six hung out on the salt-white beach of the Maya Hotel not far from my glamorous, rented house, hiding behind sunglasses, the blue bandana, the frayed straw cowboy hat, my thighs and feet getting fried in a Speedo racing suit I bought in the Maya's haberdashery, a hundred strangers having a whale of a good time in my company as I dully drank piña coladas at the outdoor bar, using Reinhardt's pesos now, and was vigilant for any glimpse of my father in the house on Avenida del Mar. So foul and fair a day I have not seen.

At four or so — the Mexican police had my watch — I finally took the hotel elevator up to the fifth floor and walked the hallway to the observation deck. A homely mother with a Mississippi accent was expertly explaining oceanography to her four children, otherwise I was alone up there, spying on the upstairs terrace of my white stucco house. A few floors below me a frail old woman in green pajamas and a flowing green robe leaned on a balcony with a highball glass in both hands. And there, *Hi Dad!*, was himself in my house, half a hundred yards away, staring at her in his starched white shirt and old-fashioned tie, his face tired and aching, five hundred years old, his heart full of melancholy, a fresh grief for me to handle before he withdrew into my bedroom again. My father was too much an outdoor man to stay inside the house for long, so I hung out up there on the fifth floor as the sea breeze lost fifteen degrees and the roof of the world was shingled with clouds. Twenty minutes later and Atticus was stepping down the staircase of tiered railroad ties and peering out at the constancy of the sea before going up to the terrace, where he sat with his hands knitted atop his head, a picture of misery, his mind wholly on me.

You've put him through hell, I thought. *Again and again.*

Went out to the jungle in a fulminating bus filled with hotel workers, getting off a half mile from Eduardo's and hiking in through high weeds and face rakers until Eduardo was frontally there in the path like a fastened door, a fierce machete in his hand. He asked in Spanish, "Are you a ghost?"

I told him in Spanish I wasn't.

Eduardo smiled. "Then I'm happy to see you, my friend."

I fell into my usual pattern there, knocking myself out on their whiskey, then waking so late and lazily that Eduardo's children were able to paint my face and affix green fronds to me as decoration. The heat and sun were like that of eleven o'clock. I was half-tempted to attend the funeral, Huck Finn on the half-shell, if only because it presented such a movie moment, *The Phantom of the Opera, The Hunchback of Notre Dame*: if I wanted to I could bellow from the high choir loft that this funeral should halt, it was all a horrible sham, and heads would turn and the gloom and melancholy in that holy place would change into something gloriously weird. Wisely, I headed instead to the sea and felt the high sun on my face and chest and tried to force pictures of Atticus out of my mind — my father offering prayers for me, my father painfully watching Reinhardt going into the ground. Would there be a dinner afterwards? Wasn't like him. I heard him telling Stuart and Renata he was a little off his feed. My father was a thoroughly practical man, far more like him to want to go out to the *casita*. And he'd see what others missed. Wildly panicking, I walked on all fours over high hills of rock or fought my way around them in my khakis and shoes, wrestling against the tougher swells, often flattening against a hard limestone shelf with the force of a half ton of water. I finally swam out fifty yards or so, just past the great wave breaks, finding help in an undertow that took me north and farther out to sea, where there was a change in the current, a fierce pull toward the cliffs and the gray cathedral of stone, and I floated with it until one foot touched sand and I fell and sloshed through the churning water just below my studio.

Climbed the faint earthen path up to it and forced open a front door that humidity was fastening to the frame. Everything was pretty much as I'd left it, though fallen hangers had been hung and Reinhardt's white underpants had been used to mop up blood from the floor. The kitchen still carried the hint of scorched coffee. I was halfway toward rinsing out the full pot of coffee before common sense got the better of habit. I fetched a Coca-Cola from the refrigerator and finished it as

I strolled the house hunting the giveaways and forgetfulness of my harried Wednesday night. I failed to check my off-brand tape player or even think of my feeble toss of Reinhardt's fancy shoes. And then, fully in love with my brilliance, I put the Coca-Cola can on the kitchen counter and walked out — *just try to find something there, Dad.*

That evening I took Eduardo's wife's Schwinn to the Pemex station on the highway. Telephoned Renata but Stuart answered and I hung up. Dialed my own number and heard myself saying, "Hi. You know the routine, name and number. I'll get back atcha later."

And I was about to hang up again when Renata got on the phone. "Hello?"

"You're there."

"And so is he."

"Still? Can you talk?"

"I have to turn the machine off." I heard her stab at a button and get back on. I heard fierce irritation with me in the flat tone of her voice. "Your father's sleeping. *El turista.*"

"Damn." I half-turned in the telephone booth. A handsome Texan was filling the tank of an old Volvo with high-octane gas. "Are you going to cancel his flight?"

"I'll ask tomorrow."

"Any sign of the Lufthansa ticket?"

"Nope."

"She must have lost the address. I'll have to check. You got the passport and visa?"

"I hunted everywhere."

"The *guest* room, Renata!"

"*Especially* there. I have no idea where they are."

The Texan shut off the high-octane pump and was now filling his tank with low-octane. A chemist. His wife leaned out of the office. "You want anything to drink, Grover?"

Grover focused on the gas pump. "No thanks."

"Scott?" Renata asked.

"I was thinking. I could get out of Mexico on the Harley-Davidson."

"Long trip."

"West to Villahermosa in one day. Another to go north to Tampico. And then on the third day Matamoros and Brownsville, Texas."

"Whatever," she said, plainly bored.

"Look, this is hard on me, too."

"Oh, shut up! You are so self-centered, Scott! You haven't even asked how your father is! And all he thinks about is you! Have you given a thought to what you've put him through?"

"Unfortunately, he's used to it."

"Well, I'm not," she said, and hung up.

It's the parable of the prodigal son, isn't it. There was a cattleman without cattle who had two sons, and the kid brother went to his father and asked for his inheritance, and his father divided his estate between his sons so he wouldn't go crazy with worry. And not many days later the one who thought much of himself gathered everything he owned and took a journey into a far country, and there he squandered his inheritance in wild living. And when he had wasted everything, he began to be in want, and he took a job in the fields feeding swine. But when he came to his senses he said, "I will get up and go to my father, and will say to him, 'Father, I have sinned against heaven, and in your sight; I am no longer worthy to be called your son; treat me as one of your hired hands.' " And he got up and went to his father. But while he was still a long way off, his father saw him, and felt compassion for him, and ran out and embraced him and kissed him. Luke, chapter fifteen.

Eduardo and his family went to Mass with friends on Sunday and afterward watched an orchestra play on the plaza of the parish church. When his friend was hauling Eduardo and his family back home in his truck, Eduardo saw a *joven* who he thought may have been Renaldo Cruz, hitcthhiking out here on the highway.

Enraged at hearing that, I flung myself right past Eduardo and I got hotter as I high-hurdled through the jungle, some juvenile part of me trying out the old Tarzan number, *I have had it with you, buster.* But when I got to the house, what I saw was my Harley-Davidson at the foot of the hill, and I knew it was not Renaldo but Atticus up there in the *casita,* holding things in his hands, assessing and gauging and gumshoeing, figuring out exactly how his son died, as if that knowledge would fill in all that was otherwise missing.

Went up the hill the hard way, through high weeds and pepper trees, nothing to recommend it as a hill to look down, a stroll to take, no pretty postcard view. And when I achieved the house, my father was scrabbling down the falloff above the cove with my shotgun like a staff in his hand, and he was getting out on a precarious gray lintel of stone to fetch from magenta oleander one of Reinhardt's Cole-Haan shoes. You haven't felt such heartache, seeing that sixty-seven-year-old sleuth, wholly out of his element, hunting one more clue, one further explanation, as if that were the hidden value x that would solve the algebra of his boy. And then an intuition caused him to fire a look up the hill at me and shade his fair blue eyes from the hard glare behind me. "Who's there?" he called out, and I retreated from him, fearing he'd seen my face, heading in full gallop down the hill's far side and helter-skeltering into the tangles and forget-it of jungle before I finally turned and saw Renaldo Cruz out there with us like some Aristotelian unity, himself in a fast sprint back to the highway and likely into town.

"We need to talk to him," Eduardo told me. "Renaldo needs a big healing."

Late that Sunday afternoon we got hold of Eduardo's friend's truck and went to the Pemex station, and I heaped a handful of coins by the public telephone as Eduardo tried Alejandro Cruz in the Resurrección directory. Alejandro had no idea who Renaldo Cruz was. Andalesía Cruz failed to answer, as did Armando. We huddled there inside the booth, my left ear firmly pressed to the handset, as Eduardo dialed again. Cecilia Cruz told Eduardo that Marcelino, no relation, might have a cousin by that name. Marcelino's phone was disconnected. We tried Emilio Cruz and Heriberto Cruz — no answer — and finally heard from Leticia Cruz that Renaldo was indeed her cousin, but she hadn't seen him since Easter. She thought he was staying with his uncle, Rafael. Eduardo flipped a page and hunted a Rafael in the directory, found none, and asked if Leticia knew how we could find him. She said he owned the Bella Vista bar.

"Boystown," I said.

We dialed that. Rafael was there. Yes, Rafael admitted, Renaldo Cruz was his nephew. And then he volunteered that Renaldo was in Dallas, working at a car wash.

Eduardo held his hand over the phone's

271

mouthpiece and whispered in Spanish, "He's lying."

"No fooling."

Eduardo got back on and told Rafael that the reason he was calling was that he too worked at that car wash and there was a shameful mistake on Renaldo's paycheck, he was paid way too little, his boss was so embarrassed about it that he'd begged Eduardo to be sure to get the money to Renaldo so his boss would not feel dishonored. Embarrassment and dishonor were far from my own experience of corporate America, but Rafael Cruz seemed to buy it and he gave Eduardo precise directions to his house in the *barrio*.

"Oh, so he's here?" Eduardo asked.

"Sure, for you," Rafael said.

We went there. The house of Rafael Cruz would probably have been a fixer-upper in *el norte,* but in Mexico it was far finer than I was used to, floored, hot and cold running water, in the dining room a highly glossed table and eight chairs and the familiar print of da Vinci's *Last Supper*, in the front room inherited chintz furniture, a picture of His Holiness kissing a child, a side table arrayed with family photographs, and hanging over the sofa a trite, ornately framed, black velvet painting of a toro and toreador in the fine execution of a veronica. Rafael's wife held the door for Eduardo and me, and softly took Eduardo's offered hand. Eduardo took off his

Padres baseball cap and said something polite and soothing as I heard him give his name as *Nicuachinel,* he who sees into the middle of things. Mrs. Cruz then asked, plainly in awe, if Eduardo was a shaman.

"God has made it so," Eduardo said, and then he asked Mrs. Cruz where Renaldo was, for we were hoping to meet him face-to-face. She hollered, "Renaldo! A shaman is here! Where are you?"

Renaldo edged in from the hallway, in blue jeans and a Dallas Cowboys jersey, a gun in his hand. The gun hung by his thigh, his first finger in the trigger housing, but he held it like a half-forgotten auto part, *You know where this belongs?* But we were like cobra and clarinet, that gun and I, a bright .357 magnum six-shot revolver. His aunt told Renaldo she hated that thing, but Eduardo gave no sign that the gun was even an affront to good manners, he simply put his Padres cap back on and urged Renaldo to have our friendly talk outside so Mrs. Cruz would not be upset.

We sat in frazzled lawn chairs under a shade tree, on hard-baked earth fenced in rabbit wire, Renaldo holding the gun in both hands between his knees, his soft, lady-killer eyes shying from mine as he asked in Spanish, "Where's my money?"

Eduardo told Renaldo he was lying about the

money, and he grinned as if the kid would find that funny. And Renaldo *did* grin. *Wow! Lying! Good joke.* "I have come here to talk for my friend," Eduardo told him.

Renaldo told Eduardo, "I have been in his house. I have seen his father. I have urinated on the floor."

Eduardo frowned. "I have told you he is my friend. Have some respect."

Children were playing with plastic trucks in the yard next-door, and an older girl in a pleasing sundress was watching a piano of ribs sizzle on the barbeque. I was finding it hard to be afraid of the murderer far to my left.

"You are trying to kill him," Eduardo said. "We know this. You have killed another man by mistake." Eduardo shrugged. "Easy to do. Both are Anglo and blond, blue eyes, it's confusing."

Renaldo nodded and scowled at the *rubio*. I hung my head and folded my forearms on my thighs, like a fatigued and sour teenager hating being out with the old folks.

"You see, though," Eduardo said. "You *have* killed the right person. The Devil himself." Eduardo turned to me. "His name was?"

"Reinhardt Schmidt."

"Sh-meet, *he* is the one who killed Carmen. My friend here, he loaned the Devil his car and on the highway there was the tragedy. But you have revenged your Carmen, you see, Renaldo?

She is happy in Heaven. She prays for you."

Renaldo shifted his gun from hand to hand as he focused on a fat red sun settling into a hatch-work of trees. "I have no reason to live," Renaldo said.

Eduardo considered him solemnly. "You are young!" he said. "You have a full life ahead of you! Your fiancée will enjoy watching it!"

The family next door followed their platter of ribs inside. Renaldo was silent. We all stared at the sun until it was nothing but a bloodline in the trees.

"Are we agreed?" Eduardo finally asked. "You won't try to kill him?"

Renaldo looked at me full-on and said, "Your friend, I feel it in my heart when he talks."

Eduardo let me off in front of Stuart's villa and I skulked around to a dining room window where I saw my father sitting in pestered silence, his hands on his thighs, as Stuart held forth on subjects he had no interest in. I'd hoped to talk to Renata, but that would be impossible with Atticus there, so I bought a six-pack of Coronas from the kitchen help at The Scorpion and strolled down to the *playa* and watched the flying stars while lying on sand that was still hot from the sun. I fell asleep after gulphing three beers and woke up to find no hint of light in Stuart's villa. I peed against a tree and peered in at the green neon of a kitchen clock, seeing it was past four.

Walked up the shoreline to my house and found it dark and took off my huaraches, then shifted the pool door an inch at a time until I fitted through. I held my breath and listened. The house was talking but that was all.

Eased up the stairs and inside the guest room, hunting for my passport and visa, and figured Atticus had to have it, he possibly had the Lufthansa ticket, too. My bedroom door was a few inches ajar, the habit of a father who listened for his wild boys to get home before he fully slept. I forced myself to push the door further and walk in. And there he was in skewed and twisted pajamas, wracked with cares, his mouth half open, his frail eyelids fluttering, who knew what horror film he was viewing? I held my hand so close to his face I felt his breath and probably shaded his fitful dreams. *Wake him now, talk to him,* some forthright and graced part of me thought, but to be fully seen, to confess what I'd done and failed to do seemed too hard, too shaming, far easier to put it off. And I did, hunting the room oh so carefully, a hand touching down here and there with the softness of a falling leaf, frightened of any sound, and finding in that way not anything I wanted, but only his gold-rimmed reading glasses and a shirt-pocket notepad with a pen underneath its front flap, as if he'd been jotting things down just that day. Even the key for the motorcycle was gone, probably in my father's trousers, and I feared coins would clink if I lifted his trousers from the chair.

Took the notepad with me downstairs and into the kitchen where I flipped it open under the hood light over the stove. Handwritten there were:

> Shirts.
> Rug gone where?
> Lufthansa ticket.
> Shoes.
> 4 shells in gun.
> Who's R.?

I frankly admit it: hot tears filled my eyes. My father was fact-conscious, observant, even omni sometimes, but his fragmented piecing together of what had happened Wednesday night was far less impressive to me than that he'd so relentlessly sought a solution. I felt humiliatingly unequal to his faithfulness, his loyalty, his love, as if I were heir to some foreign genes that my father had no part in. I hit the hood light to turn it off and in full fool fashion hit the hood vent fan instead, hitting it off again after half a second, then hitting the light switch, too. But the fan roar had been enough. I held myself still and heard the floor creak under his feet, saw the hallway flush with light, and then heard Atticus walk the upstairs, hunting the stranger who woke him.

I hurried out of the house and hushed closed the pool door, and then I just stood far away by a tide pool, fixing my gaze on the upper rooms as my father washed and dressed, fixing my gaze on the kitchen window as he ate a bowl of corn-flakes by the sink.

Atticus heaved the pool door and hammered it shut and I held my position out of his sight as he walked past, half-smiling for once, with the Radiola playing the frantically cheerful maríachi music on my homemade Linda Ronstadt tape. I heard no more, I got out of there, hurtling through sand and high grasses to the Avenida, and then walking in the faint gray of predawn until I was in the *centro.*

Had a flan and Nescafé at a hole in the wall behind the *parroquia,* but as I sat there trying to read a found newspaper, all I could think of was my father, my pursuer, hunting down clues to my murder. *Look at what you are putting him through. You can't go on like this.*

At ten I walked across the public square, ambling under the loggia and right inside Printers Inc. Renata was stacking paperbacks in a bookcase, but she let them flop to the floor in her shock at finding me there.

She glanced to the bookstore office. Stuart was fully absorbed in fiddling with his computer. "Are you *crazy?*"

278

"Worn out."

"You heard about Renaldo."

I felt I was falling. "What now?"

She told me Renaldo Cruz was shot with his own gun in his uncle's Bella Vista bar after Renaldo had harangued Rafael for half the night and finally insulted his wife. Self-defense, the police called it. "But it was suicide," she said.

My mother, first. Then Carmen Martínez. Reinhardt Schmidt. Renaldo Cruz. I forced open a pocket knife of a smile. "Who's next?"

She walked forward and fell into me with a kind of relief, holding whatever affection and faithfulness she had hard against me, her face firmly pressed to my chest, inhaling the smell of my hand-me-down shirt. She told me that the friends of Colorado State Senator Frank Cody got through the Mexican bureaucracy far better than Stuart could have, and that Reinhardt Schmidt was being exhumed in an hour or so in preparation for his shipment to Colorado. She and Stuart would have to be there to identify the remains.

"Tell them it isn't me. I have two gold fillings on my teeth. Reinhardt doesn't. You can say you just remembered."

"Oh, Scott. Are you sure?"

"I'll be fine," I said.

"Where will you go?"

"To jail, probably."

Without turning, Stuart called from the office,

"Renata? Who's there with you?"

I held her face in my hand. "Kiss me," I said, and she did. I felt the fleeting, soft give of her mouth against mine, and then I walked out the front door.

Sergeant Espinoza, my old friend from my *borracho* days, was sitting on the front steps of the police station, and he stood up with concern when he saw my face. But a Marriott van full of fresh tourists halted in the street, separating us, and when Espinoza got around it, I had disappeared underground.

Then I waited; it was the one good and tenacious thing I'd done, that waiting. I handed out my sunglasses, bandana, and frayed cowboy hat to whomever would take them and watched Stuart's beggar go out for his rounds in my gray Stanford T-shirt. Cicadas chirred in the hedges outside. A gray scorpion inched up an adobe wall and curled its poisonous tail in defense when I lightly tapped its head with a pen. A hunched old woman shuffled by as if her sole purpose was to stir up the fine, powdered earth with her shoes. An hour passed, then half of another. Even in daylight the great room was all shade and absence, as if spirit and qualities had been subtracted from it. You'd paint it in funeral black, raw umber, sienna brown, vermilion. Caravaggio colors. Colors of loss and impermanence. I was in the belly of the whale, I was with Lazarus in the tomb.

A hard rain of sunlight sheeted in when the first-floor door opened. And Atticus was there, just as I knew he would be, his face full of pursuit and worry. His hand flowed along the railing as he found his way down into that huge sepulchre and walked uncertainly across the floor, his head turning right and left as he took in the underworld all around him. I got to my feet, got over against a wall, still unsure if I would be willing to talk to him or be seen. But there was a kindliness to him, that "You okay?" look, and I found it in me to walk forward. And I asked, "Will you forgive me?" And I felt forgiven even as I said it.

SEVEN

Way back in the room, Sergeant Espinoza was taking the stairsteps one at a time. Looking fiercely in their direction. But Atticus was past caring about that future; that was only government and paperwork. His shifty second son was there, found and alive, and if there was hurt in his face and he seemed to have visited every room in hell, it hardly mattered now; Atticus was flooded with joy. He'd had his mind set on just the one thing and got surprised by the far better. "Will you forgive me?" Scott had said. Words wouldn't half do it, so Atticus hugged his son hard against himself. Wanting to fill him up with his love. "I feel like hitting ya," he finally told him.

"You'll have to stand in line," his son said.

But the gift of him was too huge. They just held each other for a while, until his son was real real to him. And then Sergeant Espinoza was there, talking to Scott in a hurried Spanish that Atticus couldn't get the hang of. At one point his son said, "Reinhardt Schmidt," and the sergeant had him write the name down.

Renata walked into the front lobby of the police station right after Scott and the sergeant went into an interrogation room. Atticus listened to them both talking reasonably in Spanish. "Everything's going to get even harder," Renata said.

"Like as not," he said. "What's the word for lawyer?"

"*Abogado.*"

"I'll have to hire a good *abogado.*"

Renata was grief itself. She said, "I'm sorry I had to lie to you."

"Well, you told the truth, mostly."

"I left a lot out."

"We do that."

She got them Coca-Colas from a machine. She told him, "When I was in college I read a folktale about a father pursuing a son who'd run far away, from one world to the next. The father called to him, 'Please come back!' But his son looked across the great gulf between them and shouted to him, 'I can't go that far!' So his father yelled to his son, 'Then just come back halfway!' But his boy replied, 'I can't go back halfway!' And finally his father shouted, 'Walk back as far as you can! *I'll* go the rest of the way!' "

Atticus flashed a smile that quickly faded. "Nice story," he said.

* * *

Scott Cody was to be arraigned for the murder of Reinhardt Schmidt and was jailed until the Wednesday court hearing. Atticus hired a good *abogado* and got on the phone with Frank, then he and Renata had found the family of Carmen Martínez. Renata helped him explain what his son did and did not do. Atticus took care of them, and then they found the family of Renaldo Cruz, and he took care of them, too.

Renata drove him to the house in silence, and then she said, "You'll have a full-time job fixing things for Scott."

"Well," he said, "you do what you can."

Reinhardt Schmidt was not his real name, he wasn't from Germany and no one sought him. It was like they made him up.

On Wednesday, the lawyer argued there was only a faulty police investigation of the murder of Reinhardt Schmidt and only tainted evidence of the *norteamericano* having been involved in trying to hide it, and he got the charges against Scott Cody reduced to failure to report a homicide. But in agreeing to the bargain, the prosecution insisted that he be sentenced to prison time for that crime, and so he stayed in jail.

Renata arranged for Atticus Cody's first-class flight from Cancún to Dallas to Denver, and he

284

went to say good-bye to his son. Scott was hunkered in his cell, a flat board on his knees, filling a Scribe spiral notebook with his handwriting. Seeing his father's sadness, he said, "You look glum."

"I guess my face got frozen like that."

Scott got up and held on to the iron bars as he tried to persuade his father not to feel sorry for him, the days were flying by, his stays in the hospital taught him how to be a good prisoner. "I have a cell of my own and plenty of time to sketch and write and play chess with Sergeant Espinoza. Renata will visit off and on; María will bring me dinner; I'm going to be teaching a class in English. I have friends here. This is the happiest I've been."

Atticus praised him with a mellow stare. "I have a ticket for your flight to Colorado."

Scott thought for too long. "We'll see."

Little Jennifer had fallen and lost a front tooth. Kids had climbed up on the horsehead pump next to the highway and sloppily painted the name of their high school on it. The Antelope truck stop was so full of talk of Mexico that Atticus stayed away for a week, and when he went there again the older people at least seemed to have gotten his point. Without a hint of prior illness, his friend Earl died in his hardware store in late March, and Atticus was a pallbearer at his funeral. The governor appointed him to a fish and game board in April, and he was re-elected to the parish council at St. Mary's. He put new shoes on the horses and helped Frank and Merle and Butch and Marvin give shots to the cattle, and at night he fell asleep with opera on the radio and a book of history in his hands.

Looking for the flush of a second bloom from his wife's perennials, Atticus got his sheep shears and knelt in the garden in June, cutting back the penstemon, rockcress, stork's-bills, and daisies. A soft rain began to fall as he heaped the green clippings on gunnysack and hauled it out back to his compost pile, and then he heard a far-off car on the highway. Why, he didn't know, but Atticus walked to the front yard, taking off his gloves, and he saw a yellow taxi heading toward the house. And while his son was still a long way off, his father rushed out to greet him.

Wild Rescue books are published by Stone Arch Books
A Capstone Imprint
1710 Roe Crest Drive,
North Mankato, Minnesota 56003
www.capstonepub.com

First published by Stripes Publishing Ltd.
1 The Coda Centre
189 Munster Road
London SW6 6AW

© Jan Burchett and Sara Vogler, 2012
Interior Art © Diane Le Feyer of Cartoon Saloon, 2012

Library of Congress Cataloging-in-Publication Data
Burchett, Jan.
[Poacher peril]
Poacher panic / written by Jan Burchett [and] Sara Vogler ; illustrated by Diane
Le Feyer ; cover illustration by Sam Kennedy.
p. cm. -- (Wild rescue)
Originally published under the title Poacher peril. London : Stripes, 2009.
ISBN 978-1-4342-3286-1 (library binding)
ISBN 978-1-4342-4195-5 (pbk.)
1. Twins--Juvenile fiction. 2. Brothers and sisters--Juvenile fiction. 3. Sumatran
tiger--Juvenile fiction. 4. Wildlife conservation--Indonesia--Sumatra--Juvenile
fiction. 5. Poaching--Indonesia--Sumatra--Juvenile fiction. 6. Sumatra
(Indonesia)--Juvenile fiction. 7. Adventure stories. [1. Twins--Fiction. 2. Brothers
and sisters--Fiction. 3. Tiger--Fiction. 4. Wildlife conservation--Fiction. 5.
Poaching--Fiction. 6. Adventure and adventurers--Fiction. 7. Sumatra (Indonesia)-
-Fiction. 8. Indonesia--Fiction.] I. Vogler, Sara. II. Le Feyer, Diane, ill. III.
Kennedy, Sam, 1971- ill. IV. Title.
PZ7.B915966Pn 2012
823.914--dc23   2011025524

Cover Art: Sam Kennedy
Graphic Designer: Russell Griesmer
Production Specialist: Michelle Biedscheid

Design Credits: Shutterstock 51686107 (p. 4-5),
Shutterstock 5161464 (p. 148-149, 150, 152)

Printed in China by Nordica
1114/CA21401697
102014   008591R

POACHER PANIC

J. BURCHETT & S. VOGLER

STONE ARCH BOOKS
a capstone imprint